JUNGLE QUEST

For several months, the British and European security agencies in Africa have been intercepting coded secret radio messages that are being received and responded to by a radio station hidden in the almost impenetrable depths of the Congo jungle. It's clear that some dastardly international plot is afoot. A top agent is despatched to investigate, but his reports cease abruptly, and weeks pass without further communication from him. So renowned jungle explorer Rex Brandon is hired to head an expedition to locate and neutralise the danger . . .

Books by Denis Hughes
in the Linford Mystery Library:

DEATH WARRIORS
FURY DRIVES BY NIGHT
DEATH DIMENSION
BLUE PERIL
MURDER FORETOLD

DENIS HUGHES

JUNGLE QUEST

Complete and Unabridged

LINFORD
Leicester

First published in Great Britain

First Linford Edition
published 2017

A catalogue record for this book is available
from the British Library.

ISBN 978–1–4448–3455–0

Published by
F. A. Thorpe (Publishing)
Anstey, Leicestershire

Set by Words & Graphics Ltd.
Anstey, Leicestershire
Printed and bound in Great Britain by
T. J. International Ltd., Padstow, Cornwall

This book is printed on acid-free paper

1

Footprint Puzzle

Rex Brandon cuffed his sun helmet to the back of his head and wiped his steaming forehead with the sleeve of his bush-shirt. Never had he known the torrid heat of the Congo forests to be so vicious as it was at the moment. Pausing in the narrow forest path, he glanced round, seeing the snake-like line of his dozen bearers as they tailed along in his wake. Even they were feeling the heat. They moved slowly, every step a labour in itself. The bundles and packets balanced on their heads dipped and swayed as they walked. Immediately following Brandon came Impo, a giant native who had come with Brandon from the distant Limpopo country, where he had acted as leader on safari for the famous geologist and big-game hunter. Now he grinned as he met his employer's eyes.

'The jungle will be glad to be rid of us, *bwana*,' he said. 'It breathes with steam for us.'

Brandon gave Impo a grim smile in return. 'Never known it so hot, Impo,' he grunted. His voice was almost drowned by the incessant chatter of the small life that moved around and above their heads. Millions of insects buzzed and pinged past Brandon's ears; the upper branches of the dense tangle of tree growth was alive with chirping birds and screeching, screaming monkeys; in the underbrush on either side of the jungle path there was constant movement, furtive and stealthy, as small unseen creatures scuttled here and there on their own mysterious business. But the earth itself, and the trees that covered it, gave forth no sound of their own. Only the ever-present blanket of equatorial heat rose in waves around the small safari party as it moved on its way.

The light was dim, for the trees overhead, entangled as they were with the living ropes of lianas, shut off all view of the blazing sky. Brandon led his men through a realm of green twilight. It was soft and soothing to the eyes, but for some reason or other its very softness frayed the nerves. Even Brandon, accustomed as he was to the mighty jungles of the world, found these dark places in the Upper Congo Basin uncomfortable. All the forces of Nature seemed to be lined up against mere man when he dared to penetrate these secret fastnesses of greenery. The stealth and viciousness and cruelty of the wild combined in a silent, treacherous enemy that knew no equal.

Impo, walking close behind Brandon, looked about him as he had done a thousand times that day; as he did a thousand times during every day of his life. Something of the grim influence of the jungle had long ago entered his soul; it would remain there for the rest of his days.

Brandon, too, instinctively kept his eyes roving from side to side as he walked forward. He knew that his men were uneasy; they had been ever since they entered the vast world of dense foliage with its hidden, slinking dangers.

Brandon pushed on laboriously, the sweat pouring down his face in streams. His hands were clammy, and the high-power rifle he carried was a dead weight. His cartridge belt was a drag round his waist. Though he kept on moving, he realised how glad he would be when it was time to call a halt and make camp for the coming night. As yet, however, it was only just after midday. Several hours of travel still lay ahead if he was to keep up the schedule he'd set himself.

The path twisted and turned as they followed it. Impo suddenly touched Brandon on the shoulder. Brandon looked round sharply. He was edgy under the heat.

'What?' he asked quietly. Impo was staring past him. His keen, dark eyes were alert as they flickered here and there.

'Sir,' he murmured, 'I see signs of men. Yonder, see?'

Brandon stiffened instinctively, tightening his grip on the stock of his rifle as he followed Impo's darting glances. 'You're right!' he grunted curiously.

The two of them started forward

hurriedly, leaving the remainder of the bearers standing in the path, resting their loads. Impo reached a spot on the path and knelt quickly, his face only inches from the ground as he examined it closely.

'Footprints, *bwana*,' he muttered.

'Local tribe, probably,' said Brandon. But something in Impo's tone put a doubt in his mind even as he spoke.

'I do not think so,' answered the native. 'This is pigmy country, sir. These prints are of a man who goes barefoot, but they are not those of one of my brothers.'

Brandon blinked. The implication of Impo's words did not reach him. 'What is that you say?' he grunted.

'These prints are too narrow,' replied Impo. He moved on, bending to examine other tracks. Brandon, peering over his shoulder, began to realise what he was getting at. The imprints of the bare feet were large, those of a fully grown man, but they lacked the broad, spread-out shape of a native's foot. The natives, who walked barefooted from babyhood, had wide feet. These were narrow, like those of a man who was used to wearing shoes.

The eyes of the two men met and held. Brandon's framed a question. Impo nodded. Then: 'These are the prints of a white man, *bwana*,' he murmured. He straightened up and shrugged his massive shoulders. 'It is what I think from what I read in the sign. That is all.'

Brandon grunted and thrust his hat back, mopping his streaming brow for the hundredth time. Then his eyes narrowed as he stared into the green wall of the jungle around them. 'Impo,' he said, 'the river for which we are heading is still some way distant, but there is a smaller river close at hand. We will make camp where we are; then you and I will follow these tracks and find out what manner of white man walks in the Congo jungle barefoot.'

Impo nodded quickly. 'It is well, sir,' he answered. 'I will see to it immediately.'

Brandon nodded as Impo turned on his heel, giving orders to the rest of the men. They, tough as they were, welcomed the respite and set about the making of camp with a ready will.

Brandon himself chose the actual site for the camp, but his eyes were continually straying to the path ahead where he and Impo had seen the prints of a man's feet. Curiosity was nagging at his brain, so that he was eager to be out on the trail by the time Impo reported everything ready.

'Good!' he said. 'Come along then. Let's find out who the jungle dweller is and what he's doing in these parts. I have a hunch that it may be an interesting business!' He grinned at Impo.

Impo shrugged, not wishing to commit himself. He was used to his employer's impetuous eagerness, his tireless energy and his uncanny skill at picking up the threads of adventure and weaving them together before they were finally unravelled. If this chance discovery of footprints proved to conceal any mystery, then Brandon would go on to its final solution. Brandon might be an expert geologist — it was to collect some rare examples of ore that he was journeying through the forests of the Congo — but he was also a born adventurer.

Brandon took his rifle, a revolver, an

ammunition pouch, and a water canteen. Impo carried a second weapon. They set off as quickly as they could. The remainder of the bearers watched them go, heads nodding and shaking as they muttered among themselves. There were times when they did not understand the whims of the white man. This was one of those times.

It was not a difficult task to follow the tracks of the barefoot man, for the ground in the jungle was soft enough to take a good impression. The line of prints continued along the well-defined path for almost a mile before altering direction, then they dived in amongst the under-growth so that Impo had to use all his skill as a tracker to follow them at any speed.

'Whoever this man is, there doesn't seem to be anything wrong with him physically,' said Brandon. 'He came striding along through this stuff as if he'd been born to it.'

Bending low to avoid the curtains of liana that hung in their way, they pressed on hurriedly, forcing a way through the thorn brush till at length Impo held up his hand as he came to a halt. 'The man slows down here,' he said. 'I think perhaps he is getting near his hut.'

'Take it easy then,' advised Brandon. 'We don't want to scare him off. Better to watch for a while before we show ourselves when we run him to earth. How old are the tracks, Impo?'

'Three or four hours, sir. No more.'

Brandon nodded. The forest stifled him, but he was now completely engrossed in the mystery that chance had laid at his feet.

The two of them moved forward again, parting the bush with caution as they crept ahead. Fifty yards further on the undergrowth thinned abruptly, giving place to a broad round clearing carpeted in short, lush grass. The place was like a bubble in the forest, for the mighty trees still met above and cut off all trace of sunlight; there was only a lightening of the greenish glow through which Brandon and his companion advanced.

On the edge of the clearing they halted, peering ahead with a curious stare. In the centre of the clearing stood a single *mopani* tree, its boughs branching out and climbing up to join the tangled mass of foliage high above. Built on a platform resting on the lower limbs of the *mopani* tree was a neat little hut. It seemed to cling to the tree like a leaf-covered growth. Everything was very still as the two men took in the scene.

'White man's hut, *bwana*,' said Impo in a whisper. 'Not a native one; too crudely made for that.'

Brandon nodded silently. He crouched on the very edge of the clearing, his keen eyes darting this way and that as he studied the picture. There was no sign of life to be seen.

'Maybe the man went somewhere else, sir,' said Impo.

Brandon considered for a few moments, watching the hut as he did so. His curiosity was getting the better of him; it became imperative that he should discover exactly who and what this strange man might be. As yet unseen, the unknown man was already cloaked in mystery. Some of the mystery might have grown from Brandon's own mind, but it was there for all that. White men — if white man it was — did not go barefoot in the Congo jungles without good reason. It was the reason as much as anything else that intrigued Brandon.

'We'll wait five minutes, Impo,' he said quietly. 'If he doesn't show up at the end of that time, we'll come out of hiding and see if he's around.'

Impo gave a nod, then sat back on his haunches, his arms hanging down between his wide-spread knees in an attitude of watchfulness. His eyes never left the hut in the tall *mopani* tree.

Brandon, while he, too, watched the clearing, let his mind rove back over the preceding weeks. It had been a highly successful trip from his point of view; the International Convention for which he had undertaken the prospecting safari would be well pleased with results. In the packs of the men who had accompanied him were rich samples of various ores. They were to be handed over to a group of scientists and United Nations representatives when he reached Ruchuru at the borders of Uganda, Tanganyika and

11

the Belgian Congo country.

Brandon hoped to make the rendezvous within a couple of days. He wondered whether this delay would make very much difference. Even if it did, he still had every intention of discovering what he could about the mysterious man whose tracks he and Impo had found.

The clearing in the jungle was empty of life. In the trees all round were chatter and tiny movements. The long, trailing lianas swayed; the thorn and acacia stirred; giant tree ferns, pandanus and bamboo shoots rustled with the constant passage of birds and other wildlife. But of human beings there was as yet no sign.

Brandon glanced at his wrist watch. The five minutes he had allowed himself were almost up.

Suddenly Impo touched his arm with stealthy fingers. Brandon did not need to ask the reason. On the far side of the clearing, partly concealed by the single *mopani* tree, there was movement. In a moment it materialised in the figures of three pigmy women making their slow and cautious way from the jungle edge.

Brandon let his breath go in a gust of interest. The three small figures made their way across the clearing towards the base of the *mopani* tree. Each woman carried a wooden bowl on her head, swaying slightly under the burden. Impo cast a glance of puzzlement at Brandon, but Brandon was intent on watching. He said nothing, only pursing his lips in silence.

The women halted at the foot of the tree, looked upwards at the leaf-and-bough hut above their heads, then deposited their bowls on the ground. A moment later they backed away, bowed solemnly, and scuttled off in the direction from which they had come.

'Well I'll be damned!' grunted Brandon laconically. He met Impo's puzzled gaze. 'What do you make of that?' he demanded softly.

The native was uneasy. There was a mystery here that he did not understand. 'Bad juju, *bwana*,' he muttered. 'What is it when women of the pigmies bring food and gifts to a strange man who lives in a tree? There is something here I do not like. We should go, I think.'

Brandon hid a grim smile. 'When we've seen the man!' he answered.

With an effort, Impo forced himself to be calm. Loyalty to Brandon made him to stay where he was, but it was against his instincts to do so.

'Come on,' said Brandon firmly. 'It's high time we paid that hut a visit.'

But even before he had risen to his feet, a grunting sound reached his ears. It was followed almost immediately by a crackling of undergrowth some distance to the left. Then an oddly assorted pair of figures broke into view and headed for the *mopani* tree.

Brandon gripped his rifle more tightly as he stared in amazement. He heard Impo stifle a gasp of mingled fear and surprise, but by laying a hand on Impo's arm he stopped him from taking flight. He himself was so staggered by what he saw that for a moment he could forgive his companion for showing terror.

Striding towards the *mopani* tree was a very tall, angular man. It was difficult to tell his age exactly, but he looked to be about forty years old. His clothes were in rags and his face was heavily bearded with coarse red hair, while the hair on his head, bleached to a lighter tone by the sun and heat, fell almost to his shoulders. Slung from one arm was a sporting rifle, while a revolver was bolstered at his waist. His feet were bare, but he wore short puttees below the knees. For the rest of his strange garb a dirty rash shirt and sweat-stained shorts did service.

But Brandon found his eyes concentrating as much on the red-bearded man's companion as on the man himself. Shambling along a yard or so behind the man came the massive form of a hairy black gorilla. The animal was making short grunting noises as it moved. To Brandon's intense amazement, the red-bearded man turned his lead and snapped out a harsh command. The gorilla immediately fell silent, almost grovelling along in its master's wake. The man reached the base of the *mopani* tree, threw a contemptuous glance at the bowls of food placed there by the pigmy women, then snapped his fingers towards them.

The gorilla seemed to need no

prompting beyond the gesture. While Brandon and the terrified Impo watched, it fell on the food and cleared it. In the meantime, the man stood watching it, a sour grin on his bearded face. When the beast had finished, he gave another order to it and then began to climb to the leaf-and-bough hut in the tree. This was accomplished by means of a rope ladder woven from twisted liana strands. The man went up it with a litheness that spoke of immense muscular strength and power. There was a certain magnificence in his movements which Brandon was forced to acknowledge, though an instinctive and deep distrust towards the man was already forming inside him.

The gorilla, having finished the food in the three bowls, squatted down on its haunches at the foot of the *mopani* tree. No man could wish for a more formidable sentry and guard.

Brandon glanced sideways at Impo, who was just about as unhappy as Brandon had ever seen him. 'Stick close, Impo,' he breathed. 'We're going to pay Red Beard a visit!'

2

The Silent Battle

Impo said nothing: his loyalty to Brandon was too great to permit him to break and run as he would dearly have loved to have done. With a wordless nod, he grasped his rifle as Brandon stood up. With their eyes on the squatting gorilla at the base of the tall *mopani* tree, the two of them started out from their place of concealment at the fringe of the undergrowth.

Instantly, the gorilla's head swung round as its keen sense of hearing and scent picked up their presence. Brandon halted abruptly, his gun eased forwards alertly as he watched, simulating surprise at sight of the gorilla. It was not in his hastily formed plan to let the strange white man realise he had been under observation. Advancing again cautiously, they started forward once more, their rifles levelled as a precaution, though

Brandon did not quite know whether the gorilla would show hostility or not. At the moment it was standing at the base of the tree, great arms swinging cumbrously, head thrust forward in a definitely belligerent fashion.

They were still fifteen or twenty yards from the base of the *mopani* tree when a voice barked at them from the hut in its branches: 'Stop where you are!'

Brandon's mouth hardened for an instant. His eyes left the sentry-like gorilla and strayed upwards to the hut. Framed in a crude doorway in the side was the figure of the bearded man. His voice was strongly accented, so that Brandon realised he was a foreigner, though from what country he hailed he could not yet tell. The second fact that impressed itself on him at once was the unwavering manner in which the bearded man kept his rifle trained on them.

Brandon did some rapid thinking. He had not exactly expected such open hostility from the tree-dweller, but it was immediately plain that the man distrusted them. If the watchfulness of the gorilla was not sufficient to prove it, the rifle certainly was. 'Hello!' he called in pretended surprise. 'Aren't you being a bit on the cautious side? What is this anyway? Are you lost in the jungle or something?'

The man gradually lowered his rifle a fraction, but it was still pointing in the direction of Brandon and Impo. 'What do you want here?' he demanded tersely.

Brandon regarded him steadily across the distance that separated them. It irked him somewhat to have to look up at the man, but he kept a tight hold on his temper nevertheless. There was no sense in antagonising the fellow unduly, he thought. 'We want nothing, my friend,' he answered slowly. 'It was pure chance that brought us to this place.' He paused. 'I thought when I saw the gorilla that it was menacing the hut, but it seems I was wrong.'

The bearded man sneered. 'Trachenko will only menace those I tell him to,' he snapped. 'You will oblige me by leaving us in peace.'

Brandon shrugged, one eye on the

great hairy beast that still crouched at the base of the tree. It was obvious that its master did not wish his visitors to come any nearer. 'Very well,' he said. 'If there is nothing you require; no assistance you need, or the companionship of men, then there is nothing for us to do but withdraw.' He threw his broad shoulders back a little, staring up at the bearded man. 'I approached you as a friend, nothing more. In the wilds men are usually glad to see their fellow beings. However, if it suits you to shut yourself away from them and act like this, that's nothing to do with me.'

'It *does* suit me!' came the curt answer. 'Now go, before I order Trachenko to speed you on your way!'

Brandon said nothing. His eyes were fixed on the man's bearded features. There was some ghost of recognition in what he saw; it was as if he had seen this man before — but not with a beard, and under entirely different circumstances. Where that had been, Brandon did not know, but the notion persisted. His memory for faces was incredible, and the knowledge that he was facing a man he had probably seen in the past was a nagging challenge in itself. For the moment, however, he gave up the struggle. The man was most likely an escaped convict from somewhere, hiding up in the jungle. His mastery of the great ape he called Trachenko was superb in a way, but other men had tamed the creatures of the wild. Impo might consider it juju, but Brandon did not. 'Sorry you feel that way about it,' he said.

'Indeed. Now go from here!' The words were punctuated by little jerking movements of the threatening rifle.

Brandon shrugged. He turned to Impo. 'Come,' he said quietly. 'We are not wanted here, Impo. It is well that we carry on with our hunting and return to camp.'

The bearded man watched them in silence as they made their way towards the edge of the clearing; Trachenko the gorilla also watched them, grunting savagely until they were out of sight. A final glance over his shoulder showed Brandon that the man had lowered his rifle but was still staring after them, while the gorilla was once more squatting at the base of the tree, on guard.

Impo, openly delighted at what he considered their lucky escape, turned his head and grinned somewhat sheepishly. Brandon frowned. 'There's something phoney there,' he said. 'I wouldn't trust that man any further than I could throw his gorilla!'

'The *bwana* is very strong,' murmured Impo.

Brandon smiled thinly. 'Not as strong as all that,' he retorted. 'Come on; we may as well let him think he's scared us off completely.'

A hint of fear returned to Impo's dark eyes. 'You mean to return?' he queried hesitantly. 'Sir, there is bad juju there! I feel it in my bones!'

'So do I. All the same, I'll be coming back — later on. Let's get moving now. We know where to find Red Beard again when we want him!'

'The *bwana* is a brave man,' muttered Impo uneasily. 'For me, I shall be glad to return to camp where we do not have tame gorillas and men with red beards and rifles.'

Brandon laughed softly as he thrust his way through the dense undergrowth beyond the edge of the clearing and headed for the forest path he and Impo had previously followed. There were any number of puzzling thoughts running through his brain, but he kept them to himself, for it was plain that Impo was not in a receptive frame of mind.

Brandon was sure he had seen the bearded stranger somewhere at some time. The fact that the man was undoubtedly a foreigner should have given him a definite lead; but for all that, identity still escaped him. He decided that his acquaintance with the man had been far too short to be certain, and it was clear that if he had seen him in the past it had not been to meet him on speaking terms. Just what he was doing in the heart of the Congo jungle was a problem that teased Brandon's mind to a great extent. However, it was a puzzle that could wait to be solved.

The two of them carried on for some time in silence. They were almost halfway back to camp when Brandon came to a halt. Impo looked at him inquiringly.

Brandon had his head to one side, listening intently. He was aware of a prickling sensation at the nape of his neck. It was not the first time he had experienced such a feeling in the jungles of the world. He was as certain that he was being followed as if he could see his follower clearly.

'What is it, *bwana*?' asked Impo uneasily. He was peering round nervously in the green gloom of the jungle path.

'Don't know,' murmured Brandon softly. He turned and faced the path they had recently trodden, staring back. Nothing stirred, but he was still left with the uneasy sense of being watched. Then he shrugged and turned again. It was useless getting nervy, he told himself.

Impo looked back. As he did so, he caught his breath and grabbed at Brandon's arm. Brandon whirled round, his rifle levelled in readiness. Something was moving through the undergrowth on the edge of the path. He caught a glimpse of a great hairy shape for an instant, then it was gone again.

'Stay where you are,' he hissed at Impo.

The native stood perfectly still. Fear was written large on his features, but he nodded violently and tightened his grip on his rifle as Brandon slipped away from the path and melted into the foliage.

Moving with uncanny silence, Brandon edged back along the path. He halted again, listening with every sense alert. The sound of a stealthy movement reached his ears from close ahead. He knew now that his hunch had been right. But the fact that he and Impo were being followed by a gorilla went a long way to stiffen his determination.

Brandon stayed rigid where he stood, hardly daring to breathe. He wondered whether the bearded man was with the gorilla. If not, then the only conclusion he could reach was that the man had sent the animal after them.

Before he could frame any further questions or solutions in his mind, the foliage parted not five yards away. Brandon and the gorilla stared at one another in silence. He could have shot it where it stood, but something stopped him from using his rifle. Instinctively he knew that if he did so, the sound of the shot would warn the bearded man of what had happened. That was not in Brandon's plan, but at the same time he had no intention of being killed or followed by a tame gorilla.

While the great ape stood there, swinging its arms and peering at him, he leant his rifle against the stump of a rotten tree and slid his long-bladed hunting knife from its sheath at his waist. Then he advanced towards the gorilla with all the caution he could muster.

Never had Rex Brandon had to call on his nerves to stand such dragging seconds of suspense as the ones that followed. Trachenko the gorilla stood and stared at him, waiting till he was within reach of his enormous arms. And Brandon had to keep on advancing or back down altogether. He did not mean to do that. Now that the die was cast, there could be no turning back. He had of his own free will chosen to meet the creature with a knife instead of a gun, and that was an end to it.

With a suddenness that startled him

and almost caught him off balance, the ape gave a short squealing grunt and lurched forward, reaching out at the same time. Great clawing paws grasped Brandon's shoulder, ripping the thin material of his bush shirt to shreds. He gritted his teeth and bore in with the hunting knife, plunging it deep into the gorilla's side. The animal gave a gasping sigh, but its grip on Brandon did not relax. In fact a moment later it had secured a second hold and was slowly crushing Brandon against its chest.

Brandon knew that he must finish the fight before it fully developed. If he failed, he would be crushed and torn to death, for pain was making the ape even more savage.

The knife was plunged home again, with all Brandon's great strength behind the blow. Fighting back against the pressure of the enormous arms that entwined him, the man used his other arm in an effort to force back the animal's head. Slavering jaws were pressed forward, their great yellow teeth protruding as they snapped within inches of his face. His fingers sank deep in the flesh of the creature's throat, and again and again his knife found its mark in Trachenko's side.

Swaying and struggling together, the pair fought in almost complete silence. Brandon was gasping for breath; the gorilla grunted spasmodically at every fresh thrust of the knife. Then its grunts were weakening gradually as blood poured from a dozen wounds in its side.

With a tremendous effort of physical power, Brandon gave a terrific heave and tore himself free of the deadly grip. At the same time he lunged forward with his knife arm, sinking the blade straight into Trachenko's hairy throat. The ape flailed at him with its arms, nearly knocking him over with a single blow. It tried again and again to wrench the knife from its throat, but Brandon had rammed the point so deeply in that it was jammed between the creature's vertebrae. An instant later, Trachenko gave a final gurgling grunt and very slowly keeled over backwards, collapsing at the knees and sprawling in a mountainous heap on the ground.

Brandon stepped back a pace. He felt unsteady now that the frightful strain of that silent combat was past, but a sense of relief and triumph filled his heart as he stared at the great beast he had killed. But only for a brief moment did he allow triumph to divert his attention from any other danger that was likely to follow. Darting back to where he had left his rifle, he picked it up, peering round narrowly, half-expecting to see the bearded stranger burst into view. There was no other movement, however. He took one more look at the dead gorilla, then made his way back to the path where Impo was waiting. Impo heaved a sigh of relief at seeing his employer again, for he had heard something of the battle in the undergrowth.

Brandon beckoned him forward. 'It is dead,' he said simply. 'The white man's gorilla will not harm us now.'

Impo's eyes were wide and incredulous, but when he saw the monstrous body there was no denying what Brandon had said. Brandon himself had not escaped unscathed. He was torn and scratched in several places. They tried to extract Brandon's hunting knife from the animal's throat, but it defied their efforts.

'Leave it,' said Brandon. 'We'll send some of the others along to cut it out later on. All I used it for was to deal with the brute without letting its master know what had happened.'

'*Bwana*, I shall never cease to marvel,' whispered Impo, his eyes fixed on the dead gorilla.

Brandon muttered something, then turned away and started towards the jungle pathway again. He was anxious to get back to camp and dress his wounds before carrying on towards Ruchuru. The bearded stranger must wait, but a report should be put in about his presence in the jungle. Had Brandon been in British territory, he himself might have taken stronger action; but since he was only in the Congo with special permission, he decided that the matter could rest where it was for a time.

And it would have done had it not been for the events of the next few minutes.

He and Impo were still within sight of the dead gorilla when there was a sudden disturbance in the thorn scrub ahead. Next instant they found themselves surrounded by a score or more of pigmies. Usually a friendly race, the small natives were now in an openly hostile frame of mind.

3

'A Powerful Juju Man!'

Brandon stopped in his tracks, at first puzzled and then a little uneasy. He did not want to be forced into a fight with the men if it could be avoided, but from their present attitude it certainly looked as if they were anything but friendly. Knowing them of old as he did, Brandon was more than a little worried, for his dealings with them, once their initial shyness had been overcome, had been of the pleasantest nature.

'Stay quiet, Impo,' he warned. His eyes were darting round, realising that the pigmies had surrounded him entirely. Their spears were poised in a menacing fashion, and he saw more than one of the powerful bows and poisoned arrows they used for hunting. It was not a pretty sight, but he had been in tighter corners before and escaped unscathed.

Impo said nothing. If his employer was confident, he could accept a situation equably — even if it did stir the fear in his veins.

Brandon rested the stock of his rifle on the ground and peered round at the wrinkled faces of the natives. Then he raised his hand in friendly salute.

One of the small naked pigmies took a step forward. He gave no sign with his hand, but his spear was directed at Brandon. When he spoke his voice was alive with animosity. 'You are our prisoners,' he said. 'by the orders of my chief. You have killed the big juju man's ape. If you are his enemy, you are the enemy of all of us.'

Brandon kept his face expressionless. So he'd been right, he thought sourly. This was all due to the bearded stranger's malignant influence in the jungle. He did not like the notion, but there seemed no argument against it. 'We are your friends, not your enemies,' he said slowly. 'Give the sign of peace and let us go on our way. The ape was only killed because it attacked us.'

But the man only shrugged and jabbed closer with his spear. 'You will come with us to our village,' he said curtly. 'That is our order! What you have done is worthy of death. Do not use your white man's fire-stick or you will die.'

'So would a lot of you,' retorted Brandon grimly. 'It is not my wish to kill you or your fellows. Let us pass in peace. If you force us to fight, my man and I can kill many of you before you destroy us. What will it gain you?' His eyes were darting from side to side, adding up the chances and finding them slim. Before he could bring up his rifle or fire his revolver, the pigmy could wound or kill him with a single stab. It was not an ideal position to be in.

'We are ready to die,' said the pigmy leader. 'It is our order that you come with us to the village, where our chief will speak with you. It is he who will decide your fate. Are you willing to come? You will not be harmed if you put up no fight. That is our word.'

Brandon considered for a brief moment. It would be better to avoid bloodshed if he could possibly do so, he decided. There was always a chance that he could make the chief of the tribe see sense when they talked. It was better than throwing away his life out here in the jungle.

'Your word is good,' said Brandon. 'Do not harm us, and we will come with you to the village of your tribe. That is my promise to you.'

'It is well,' replied the small native. 'Now we go.'

Before Brandon fully realised it, he found that the pigmies had closed in on all sides of himself and Impo. Then there was a firm pressure against him, and the entire party was moving off through the density of the jungle. Brandon managed to exchange a word or two with Impo before they were separated. His headman was not overly happy, but this was a different peril to the bearded man who tamed the gorillas. For the moment, he was content to follow Brandon.

Hemmed in completely, Brandon and Impo were hustled through the undergrowth. Not one single opportunity for escape presented itself. The natives kept so close that neither of them could move hand or foot without being in spear-thrust range. Brandon could have opened fire with his gun, but he knew that no sooner had he killed or wounded one of the pigmies than the rest would cut him to pieces in a matter of seconds. Besides, he had given his word.

The path they followed was one which Brandon did not know. It penetrated deep into the jungle at right angles to the route he and Impo had previously been following. As he strode along, he wondered what the red-bearded stranger was doing; whether he would be present at the pigmy village when they reached it; what manner of man he really was to have gained such complete control over not only gorillas but men as well.

But his queries were not to be answered at once. Many strange things and many stirring adventures were to take place before Brandon finally sorted out all the strings that were woven into the mystery of the footprints in the jungle.

The pigmy village was small, dirty and straggling. It stood in a clearing on the banks of one of the lesser rivers that fed down to the growing Congo. The river was swift hereabouts, so that the danger from crocodiles to the natives was slight. Rangy-looking curs strolled unmolested among the round mud huts. Small naked children stood and stared as Brandon and Impo were herded in from the jungle and taken directly to one of the huts that was set slightly apart from the rest.

'This'll be the chief's place,' murmured Brandon.

It was true. A moment later, almost before the party had come to a halt, a wizened old man, so small as to be almost a dwarf in size, appeared from inside the hut. He was leaning heavily on a tall staff as he surveyed the arrivals. Brandon returned his stolid gaze. The ghost of relief entered his mind as recognition dawned on him. He knew this pigmy chief from adventures in the past. If personal acquaintance could help their cause, it looked as if luck was coming their way after all.

Brought to a halt in front of the hut, they stood still while the leader of the little hunting party advanced and bowed before the chief. The old man raised his staff in acknowledgment, but his face remained unchanged, revealing no emotion of any kind. Brandon listened while the pigmy hunter described in detail how he and his fellows had come on the white man and his companion immediately after they had slain the gorilla. There was awe in his voice as he told of how the great ape had been killed with a knife, the blade of which was still imbedded in its carcase. The white man, despite his crime, was a mighty hunter. But he had killed the big juju man's gorilla, and that could not be overlooked.

Brandon waited as patiently as he could until the story was told. Still the old chief made no sign or comment. But his eyes dwelt on Brandon for a long time when his hunter fell silent. Then: 'White man *bwana*,' he murmured in a low voice, 'what I hear is bad. The bearded one's ape was his servant. He is a powerful juju man! This killing will bring misfortune on my people. The bearded one will destroy our huts because we did not give him protection as he ordered.'

Brandon took a step forward, raising his arm as he did so. From the corner of his eye he caught a glimpse of Impo edging closer up behind him. He hoped he would not try anything foolish.

'Great Chief,' he said quietly, 'it is bad that you and your people should show a visitor such enmity. I did not come to your country to kill or harm you or your people. I was forced to slay the gorilla because it was my life or his. If a man is faced with a charging elephant that belongs to another, do you say that he must not kill it? Would you have him stand and wait for death simply because that animal is another man's property? Great Chief, that is the talk of a man not so wise as yourself.' He paused, waiting to see if his words would have any effect.

The old chief blinked his rheumy eyes but he did not speak for several seconds. When he did, his voice was less curt, more gentle and friendly. 'White man,' he said solemnly, 'what you say is true in most cases; but this is different. The bearded one is a powerful man. His word is law to us, just as his word is law to the creatures of the wild. I am in a very unhappy position now, for I see in you an old friend.'

Brandon permitted himself a smile. 'Many times have we hunted together, Great Chief,' he reminded the man. 'I have come and gone in your country with friendship before. How is it that your hunters threaten me with death this time? Is there not something I can do to make you see what folly this is?'

The old man shook his head sadly. Then he suddenly squared his stooping shoulders and waved his staff in a sign of dismissal to the group of natives gathered at the backs of the prisoners. 'I will speak with the white man in my hut!' he said. 'Go!'

Brandon heaved a sigh of relief. This was a good sign, he decided. The chief's determination was weakening. 'It is well,' he said. 'We are friends, and friends can talk wisely together.'

'Even enemies can talk,' returned the chief enigmatically. He turned and led the way into the dim interior of the hut at his back. Brandon and Impo followed respectfully. Both men still carried their guns, for no attempt had been made to disarm them. Either the pigmies had accepted their word and trusted it, or they did not realise the possibility of a sudden attack. However, there was no question of Brandon or his companion turning on the old chief.

The chief indicated that they should sit down on the beaten earth floor of the hut. He clapped his hands and some food was brought; also a sickly drink which was taken from gourds and passed round liberally. During the whole of the repast, no word was spoken about the reason for Brandon's presence in the village. Not until a servant had removed the remains of the meal and the visitors had shown their appreciation in the accepted manner did the chief broach the subject again.

'I am fearful for the safety of my people,' he said very quietly. 'The bearded one has powerful juju and will be angry when he finds that the big gorilla is dead.'

Brandon cleared his throat and threw a warning glance at Impo. Impo said nothing; he decided to leave all the talk to his employer.

'Chief,' began Brandon gravely, 'tell me who this bearded one is and where he comes from. Why are you and your brave people afraid of him? He is not anyone to whom you owe allegiance. He is nothing but a lone man living in the jungle. Probably he is hiding from the law.'

The old chief looked at him keenly. 'It is easy to speak thus, *bwana*,' he answered. 'What you say is true in a way. The bearded one is not known to us as you are; but we fear him. He controls a herd of gorillas as I control my own hunters! He must have very powerful juju medicine.'

Brandon compressed his lips. 'His medicine will make you sick if you take too much of it, Great Chief,' he said. 'Suppose your hunters had slain me when they found us by the dead gorilla — what would have happened then, eh? White men would have sent many men with guns and taken revenge for our death. The bearded one could not have saved you and your village by his juju. This is foolish talk, oh Chief. Tell me what I ask now.'

The old man hesitated. He was obviously disturbed by Brandon's reasoning, but fear sat large in his eyes as he stared back at the white man. 'I will tell you what I can,' he replied quietly.

'When did this bearded one come to your country?' asked Brandon.

'Several moons ago, *bwana*. A great bird-machine making much noise and frightening my people crossed the sky one night when the moon was at the full. We took it as an omen of evil.' The old man paused uneasily, glancing round as if he expected to see the bearded one rise up and smite him. Then he continued in little more than a whisper: 'My hunters found the bearded one several days later. He had built himself a hut in the great *mopani* tree and was living there. When my hunters approached, they were attacked by one of the gorillas. The bearded one watched from the tree, but it was not until my men were almost defeated that he saved them by commanding the gorilla to leave them in peace. How he did it, *bwana*, is a mystery that I cannot understand, but he spoke in the language of the apes, and the animal

43

obeyed as a man would do.

'Since then we have sent him food, for he ordered us to do so. He speaks sometimes of the great day when all our people will be released from the yoke of the white rulers across the sea to whom we pay homage. He makes us promises, and tells us that if we obey him the time will come when a mighty bloodshed will happen and the native races will rule the country as they did in the past. That is all I can tell you, *bwana*, and I am afraid for having told what I know; but you have been my friend in the days of old and the tie is strong. Now you must leave this place and never say a word of what I have spoken. If you do, my people will suffer under the bearded one.'

Brandon considered all he had heard. He was inclined at first to put the red-bearded man down as a fanatical madman who had chosen the jungle as a home in preference to life in the cities; but it was the chiefs mention of a plane that made him pause and wonder. Possibly it was nothing more than a coincidence that an aircraft had passed over just before the bearded man made himself known to the pigmies. On the other hand, there could be a much more sinister meaning behind it. At the moment, however, he could not quite line it up with the facts he knew.

He rose to his feet and stood looking down at the wrinkled old chief. 'Have no fear, my friend,' he said quietly. 'Your concerns and your secret are safe with us, who respect you. Now I and my man will leave your village in peace. If we come again it will be as friends, as it always has been before.'

The chief, too, rose. There was a smile on his face. 'It is well, *bwana*,' he said. 'I did not want to kill you, though my people would have done so willingly, for they fear the bearded one even more than I do. You must leave here now, and may fortune go with you.'

Brandon acknowledged the words in a suitably grave tone. Then he and Impo were escorted from the hut by the chief and led to the edge of the village. On the chief's orders, one of the hunters of the tribe accompanied them for some way till they were well clear of the village. Then they headed as fast as they could for the spot where their own camp had been established.

'I'm going to put in a report about this bearded one,' said Brandon to Impo. 'The man is probably an escaped convict, or a little mad or something, but he may do a lot of damage before he's through unless something's done to stop his tricks.'

'The *bwana* is wise,' said Impo placidly. Brandon grunted wordlessly. He was frowning as he turned things over in his mind. 'He may be something else entirely,' he added thoughtfully. The words made Impo throw him a glance, but it was plain that he did not understand what lay behind Brandon's remark.

'Rig the radio up as soon as we get back to camp,' said Brandon. 'I want to send word to Ruchuru.'

'It shall be done, sir,' was the answer.

Arriving at camp, Brandon set about the writing of a message for transmission on the small compact portable unit he had brought along with him. When Impo had seen to the setting up of the station,

Brandon called the little headquarters at Ruchuru for which he was making. No sooner had the crackle of static died away as he tuned in before he was listening to the voice of the man on the other end.

'Rex Brandon?' asked the man. 'Return here at once. It's a matter of the utmost urgency. Important meeting.'

4

Rumours

Brandon answered the message, checking back deliberately. Then he intimated that he himself had a message to pass on.

'Sorry, old man,' said the man on the other end, 'but we're terribly busy here. Awful flap going on. Unless your message is vital, will you please keep it till you come yourself? Don't like to ask you, but that's the way it is. I'm on my own here at the station and can't run errands. You do understand, don't you?'

Brandon said he did. After all, the story about the strange bearded man in the jungle was not of the first importance. But he was sorely puzzled as to the urgency of his recall. He was already on his way to Ruchuru, and could not get there much sooner than he had planned. Nor was there anything to be gained by questioning the operator at Ruchuru radio station. The man was obviously in a hurry to be rid of him, so he did not prolong the conversation.

Calling Impo, he learned that a meal was ready for them. The rest of the men had, of course, eaten theirs long ago. 'We leave here the moment we've finished,' said Brandon. 'Have everything loaded up and packed while we eat. Urgent message from base.'

Impo blinked, but made no comment.

Brandon hurriedly finished the meal that had been prepared during their absence, then he checked his guns and stood watching the final preparations for moving off.

Impo, coming up beside him, grinned. 'There are two or three hours of daylight left yet, *bwana*,' he murmured.

Brandon nodded. 'We'll make what time we can,' he said. 'Also, Impo, I'm anxious to get away from the vicinity of the red-bearded stranger and his gorillas before they strike at us again and cause delay. I'll settle with that gentleman at a later date!'

'Yes, *bwana*.'

A minute or two afterwards they were off, moving on down the narrow jungle path at a fast pace, the bearers strung out behind.

They camped that night several miles nearer to Ruchuru. Brandon was satisfied with his progress, and calculated that by the evening of the following day they ought to be within sight of the little township where he was due to rendez-vous, and where, apparently, something of importance was happening. His curiosity was fully aroused by the remarks of the radio operator, but the man had not been able to give him details.

On the move again before dawn, Brandon forced the pace to the limit. The men did not complain, for they respected Brandon and knew that he would not be driving on through the forest in this way without good cause. Though they were ignorant of the reasons behind his speed, they were ready enough to give of their best when he called on them.

It was somewhere round noon when he led his party into a large clearing on the banks of one of the many Congo River tributaries that sprang from the distant hills. Halting abruptly, a slow grin spread across his suntanned features as he beheld a long file of bearers threading their way into the clearing from a northerly direction. Heading the file was the leathery little figure of a red-faced man. He was bandy-legged, loud-voiced and thoroughly disagreeable-sounding. Stray wisps of long, thin sandy hair poked out from all round his sun helmet. He carried a rifle in one hand and a fly swatter in the other, while a water bottle hung from his shoulder on straps so long that the canteen almost tripped him with every step he took.

Brandon shouted out, waving his free arm as he did so. The man halted as if he had run into a brick wall. His face puckered up, then his mouth opened and shut again.

'Hello, Mac!' bellowed Brandon. 'Where the devil did you spring from?'

The man stiffened up and hastened across the wide expanse of the clearing. Brandon was already going out to meet him. The two met in the centre, where tall savanna grass grew in profusion. 'Mac' — or McNulty, as was his full name — said nothing for the moment, but his hand-grasp was as hard as steel when he gripped Brandon and shook till his arm nearly came off. At last he found his voice.

'Och, mon!' he roared. 'If it isn't Rex! An' what are you doin' in these forsaken parts?'

Brandon grinned at the pleasant twang he knew of old. McNulty was a fellow geologist of very high standing. The two men had undertaken a considerable amount of research work together in the past, and now it looked as if they would team up for the short journey to Ruchuru, if not further.

'Ruchuru?' asked Brandon. 'You've been in the hills, of course. I almost forgot. There's a hell of a flap on by what I can gather. Urgent recall.'

McNulty nodded, frowned, and swished at a persistent fly with his swatter. 'Aye,' he said. 'I've heard somethin' meself, lad. Don't ask me what it's about, but I got a message by radio not so long back. I was making the rendezvous in any case — same as you were.' He stopped and looked round. 'Well,' he added, 'we might as well carry on now. My men seem to have met yours before by the look of it!'

Brandon saw that the bearers were talking animatedly, the two safaris inextricably mixed where they had met nearby in the clearing.

'I was thinkin' o' stoppin' for a bite to eat,' said the Scotsman thoughtfully. 'How do you fancy that now?'

Brandon thought for a moment. It struck him as a good idea. He nodded and turned to shout for Impo. The native came running, and listened while Brandon gave instructions for a hasty camp to be made and a meal prepared. 'We'll push on after dark if necessary,' he said. 'An hour here won't make all that much difference, and I caught up some distance yesterday.'

Seated together in the shade of a wide spreading *mchwili* tree on the edge of the clearing, the two men rested and talked. McNulty was a positive mine of rumoured news. He had picked up scraps of information in a dozen of the small village outposts through which he had travelled in the past few weeks. Covering a wider area than Brandon, he had been engaged on more or less the same type of work — that of collecting samples of rare mineral deposits.

Brandon, thoughtfully stuffing his pipe and lighting it, leaned back in a canvas chair and stared across the clearing to the deep green wall of the jungle beyond. 'I ran across a pretty rum character yesterday,' he said.

McNulty raised his sandy eyebrows and blinked. His face was mobile, never in repose for more than seconds at a time. 'Ah,' he murmured. 'Mon, but there's dozens of 'em in this country. Hundreds, I should say!'

'Not like this gent, though! He was using a tame gorilla for a sentry till I had to kill the brute when he sent it after me!'

McNulty sat up straight and snorted. 'Now that's verra interestin' indeed!' he growled. 'It wouldn't be a man with a great red beard and a wee sort of accent in his speech now, would it?'

Brandon grinned. 'You've described him perfectly,' he said. 'He has a rifle as well, and isn't exactly the most friendly of creatures.'

'Aye, you're right there,' answered the other man. 'Mind, I'm only sayin' what I've heard. Never met him meself, but there's rumours. Aye, there are that. Rumours!' He rolled the word round his mouth as if it tasted good.

'What sort of rumours?' queried Brandon. He could not completely hide his interest or curiosity. McNulty sensed it and seemed to slow his story down accordingly. There never was a man for holding his audience like McNulty, thought Brandon.

'Weel now, you're asking something, lad. It's been said that this man — a sort of hermit, you might call him, I suppose — can tame and control the wildest animals of the jungle.' He chuckled throatily. 'I'd like to see him try it with a mamba!'

Brandon grinned. 'Go on,' he prompted. 'He's been putting the natives under his spell as well. Have you heard about that part of it? It worries me a little.'

The Scotsman was immediately alert. 'Has he noo?' he said, drawing a deep breath. 'Well, I'd say that was verra interestin'! Verra interestin' indeed!'

'Yes; that's what I thought. His influence almost cost me my life, to say nothing of Impo's. Red Beard is no friend of mine, I assure you!'

'Why didn't ye grab him then?'

Brandon shrugged. 'I didn't want to start a string of complications, for one thing,' he murmured. 'I wasn't in my own territory. The best thing I could think of was to put it in a report and let the Belgian government deal with the matter. Not really my pigeon, and the odds are that I shouldn't be thanked for interfering where I didn't belong.'

'Hmm . . . I see your point, lad. It's a wee bit tricky, I'll admit. Ah weel, forget it till we get to Ruchuru. I hear there's some other yarn flyin' around there about a lass that's been lost in the jungle.'

'Oh? What's the yarn?'

McNulty waved his hand vaguely in the air. He still grasped his fly-whisk and had been using it tirelessly during the conversation. 'Och, one o' them film stars or such like, she is. She and some man she's working with went out on a hunting trip. The wee lass never came back.'

Brandon sighed. 'If only these inexperienced people wouldn't go wandering off on their damn fool hunting trips there wouldn't be so many of these unsolved tragedies of the wilds,' he said heavily. 'They ought not to be allowed.'

'Aye, there's truth in that, mon. I'm thinkin' that we'll be asked if we've seen anything of a white woman when we get to Ruchuru. It seems she's a famous person in her way. Film star!' He snorted derisively.

'She probably can't help it, Mac!' said Brandon with a grin. 'Doesn't matter who she is, it's pretty tough to be lost in the Congo country.'

'Aye, I'll give ye that. But still . . . ' He got up and stretched his arms. He was no taller than Brandon's shoulder, but his elfin humour and terrific personality made him a great man for all that.

'Ready to move?' queried Brandon.

McNulty nodded quickly. 'Aye, let's be goin',' he said. A moment later his voice was to be heard yelling and shouting for his bearers to break camp. Brandon got hold of Impo and issued similar orders. In less time than it takes to tell, the two safaris were moving once more, heading by as direct a route as possible for Ruchuru.

They were still some distance from the town by the time evening came down, but by mutual agreement the two leaders pushed on after dusk. The country was not entirely strange to either of them, for Ruchuru had been their starting point, so that the ground was familiar enough for them to cope with in darkness. Nor were they so hampered by jungle now, for it had thinned out into scrubland. The sky was visible, and a nearly full moon shed its pale silvery light on their path.

Presently Brandon halted, peering ahead at a faint gleam of light. 'Ruchuru,' he breathed. 'We shan't be long now.'

'Aye, you're right, lad,' answered McNulty soberly. 'An' I've a notion we'll be busy men for a time when we do get in.'

Brandon said nothing more. They plodded on, their long file of bearers stringing out in their wake. Impo walked close behind Brandon, in company with McNulty's headman, Muuma. The two were apparently old friends and talked together constantly, going over details of past hunting trips with their respective employers.

Then the town of Ruchuru received them. After the long days and weeks in the solitude of the jungle, the scattered buildings of the town seemed almost to gain the proportions of a veritable city. There were lights and noise and what appeared to be a great many people milling around in the one crowded street.

Brandon and McNulty strode along. They made a queerly assorted pair, for Brandon's magnificent physique was matched by the little Scotsman's smallness. Coming to a stop outside a corrugated iron building that served as local government headquarters, they told the men to wait. It was then that Brandon caught sight of other white men coming from the radio station to greet them. He recognised one of them as a man of great importance, both on the African continent and in world affairs. In fact, he was surprised to realise that such a V.I.P.

had deigned to grace the geological rendezvous with his presence.

'Ah, Brandon!' said the V.I.P. in a hearty tone of voice. 'Pleased to see you again. Everything all right?'

'Yes, thank you, sir,' answered Brandon with a smile. He turned towards McNulty, who seemed inclined to take a back seat for once in his life.

The V.I.P., however, was already reaching out to shake hands with the diminutive Scot. Other white men were crowding round. Many of them were well-known to Brandon and his companion, while others were foreigners to whom he was introduced and forgot for the time being. The meeting was apparently on an international scale. It struck Brandon, who had not expected anything like this crowd of important people, that Ruchuru was an odd place to pick for such a convention. There must be something of the utmost urgency in the air to account for it.

'Send your men across to the hutments, gentlemen,' said one of the minor officials. 'Everything is arranged for their accommodation. Our staff is hard-pressed, but meals can be served within the hour.'

'Admirable,' grunted McNulty. There was a faint note of cynicism in his voice. He was notoriously hostile to officialdom; in fact his life had been one long battle against it. Sometimes he had come off best; at others been abashed for his trouble. But McNulty was a fighter.

Brandon gave Impo orders, then turned expectantly to the reception committee.

The V.I.P. met his glance and smiled reassuringly. 'I know you must be tired, gentlemen,' he said, 'but I must ask you both to attend a short conference before you turn in for some well-earned rest. There are several things we must all discuss.'

No one said anything against the proposal, but followed the big man in through the door of the ugly corrugated iron structure behind him. Inside there was a large bare room that served as an office. On either side of a long table were chairs, while a table at the far end of the room held bottles and glasses. An attendant stood ready nearby. The V.I.P. suggested a drink all round before they got down to business. This done, the servant was dismissed, and silence fell while the V.I.P. looked at everyone in turn.

Brandon now had a chance to take stock of his companions. For the most part they were dried-up-looking officials and administrators. One, however, caught his attention. He was obviously British, and was probably travelling with the V.I.P. as an aide. It was clear, too, that he was an R.A.F. man. His sweeping moustache and keen eyes were evidence enough of that fact. There was, too, a twinkle in his eyes and a roving glance that brought a hint of amusement to Brandon's face. Someone spoke to the man and called him Graham. Brandon thought he would be a useful fellow to have around on safari. When he spoke, his voice was light and drawling, as if nothing in the whole world would ever worry him.

The remainder of the gathering were partly foreigners, with a few other Britishers among them. For the most part they took the present matter with a pompous air of gravity.

The V.I.P. cleared his throat. 'Some of you know why we are here,' he began. Brandon found his voice a trifle heavy. The V.I.P. looked directly at him. Perhaps he guessed what he was thinking. Brandon gave no sign, but sat relaxed in his chair, thinking that it would be great to get a bath when the meeting was over.

The V.I.P.'s next words shook him out of such dreams. 'Brandon, and you, McNulty, have been specially sent for because you know this country better than most other men. Also, you were close at hand and on your way here in any case. There is work for you both, and I know I can rely on you doing it to the best of your ability.'

He paused. Brandon eased himself in his chair and stretched his long legs out straight in front of him under the table. 'We're ready to do all we can, sir,' he put in quietly. 'I speak, I think, for McNulty as well as myself.' A glance at the Scot confirmed this.

McNulty nodded shortly, his eyes switching round the faces at the table. 'Aye, mon, we'll do whatever we can; but we canna do anything till we know what's to be done!'

The V.I.P. permitted himself a smile, then it faded as he looked down at a sheet of paper on the table before him. 'This is an unusual meeting for an unusual purpose,' he continued. He glanced up at Graham. 'I am taking it as gospel that these reports are correct,' he said.

Graham nodded. 'As near as we can work them out, sir, that is,' he added cautiously. 'Direction-finding can be very tricky under the conditions we have to cope with in this climate, you understand.'

'Quite, quite, my boy! But we'll accept them as good, eh?' He looked up at Brandon again, frowning slightly. 'Brandon,' he said, 'you've got to find a secret radio that's in operation in the jungle. Now you know why you're here!'

5

Tie-in or Tangle?

'A secret radio?' echoed Brandon, starting up straight in his chair at the words. 'But good heavens, sir, what would McNulty and I know about secret radios?'

The V.I.P. smiled somewhat bleakly. 'You may know nothing of their internal working, Brandon,' he pointed out, 'but at least you know this country. I'm not asking you to do a technician's job; don't think that. But you and McNulty are the only men available in the district on whom we can call in this emergency. Your task will be to locate the radio exactly and take steps to silence it.'

'I see,' mused Brandon. He shot an oblique glance at McNulty, who grinned broadly.

'Never imagined I'd get myself mixed up in a thing like this,' he grunted. 'Cloak and dagger, eh? Aye, mon, but it could be fun!'

'A very grave form of amusement,' observed the V.I.P. somewhat stiffly. 'But let me give you both further details.' He dropped his gaze to the piece of paper in front of him. When he met their eyes again, his face was grave. 'All this is probably news to you,' he went on. 'But to us, who work in the centre of international affairs, it is neither new nor encouraging. The future of the United Nations may well depend on the success or otherwise of your assignment. Are you ready to accept that responsibility?'

Brandon shrugged a little helplessly. 'Certainly, if you consider it safe to put it in our hands, sir. I can hardly say more than that.'

The V.I.P. glanced round at the others seated at the table. His glance almost said: *What did I tell you?* To Brandon and McNulty, he said: 'Good! Now then . . . For several months there have been a number of rumours rife in Africa. There are always rumours, we know, but these are based on facts. Coded messages have been intercepted on the air. We are fully aware of their point of origin, but it was

66

not until recently that anyone gained an idea as to where they were directed and from where the answers went out. I will not tell you where those messages came from, gentlemen, because your own intelligence should do it for me. The thing that interests us directly at this moment is that answers are being sent from a spot in the depths of the Congo jungle country.' He paused, looking round intently, his sharp eyes moving from face to face with a hardness behind them that boded no good to anyone who underestimated the gravity of the position.

Brandon cleared his throat softly. Then: 'You mean that these coded messages are being received and replied to by a man in the jungle, sir?' There was a deep note of thoughtfulness in his voice when he spoke. McNulty glanced at him curiously. The V.I.P. nodded without speaking. Brandon said: 'May I ask you something, sir?'

'By all means.'

'What steps have been taken to locate this secret radio up to now? Or are we the first to be put on its track?'

There was a moment's silence. Then: 'One of the best agents we have in any country embraced by our organisation is out there at this moment. We have not heard a word from him for several weeks, and the absence of news is beginning to worry us. His last message, received on the 28th of last month, was not over explanatory, but hinted at several worrying aspects of the business.'

'I see, sir. Was your agent a competent man when it came to working under jungle conditions?' Brandon waved his hand. 'I don't mean to cast aspersions on him, of course, but the jungle requires certain very specialised qualities in the men who travel its paths. I understand from rumour that a woman has recently been lost in the jungle. She was not used to it and it took its toll, as it has done on many occasions in the past. Do you see what I'm driving at, sir?' He put his head a little to one side and waited.

The big man smiled thinly. 'I agree, Brandon,' he answered. 'But Grainger was as much accustomed to jungle movement as you yourself are. We have not yet given up hope of his success. However, to make doubly sure, and because we have later information that we cannot pass on to Grainger, it was thought advisable to send for you and McNulty to act as a second force.'

'Fair enough,' grunted the Scot laconically. 'Well, sir, we're ready to give a hand, never fear. Can ye give us a close approximation of the position from which this radio is working? It would help a lot, ye understand.'

The V.I.P. smiled in spite of himself. 'Certainly, McNulty,' he replied. 'I have Graham's figures with me, and he assures me they are fairly accurate. The radio is working, or was working when last picked up, from an area some two or three days' march from here in the heart of pigmy country. If you are willing to go out after it, you will have the full cooperation of the Belgian government, together with the necessary licences and permits. This thing is on an international basis, you understand, and nothing will be spared if it brings about the end we have in view. That radio *must* be located, and the man who operates it captured and brought back here.' To emphasise his words, he thumped on the table with a clenched fist. There was silence when he finished speaking.

Brandon clicked his teeth together softly. 'We can start tomorrow,' he said. 'There's only a matter of depositing the mineral and ore samples we've brought back from our separate trips. That can be done very quickly and need not hold us up at all. My own party will be quite prepared to set off again at once, and no doubt McNulty's will do the same. Is there anything else you have to tell us, sir?'

The V.I.P. glanced down at his sheet of paper again. 'Only that as soon as they are available, we shall be sending out a small detachment of picked men to follow you up,' he said. 'They are not local men, but are part of a very select policing force being evolved by the U.N. for places where jungle predominates. Unfortunately they are not immediately available, or they would already have been put on this assignment. You must understand that it is highly irregular to enlist men such as yourself and McNulty here to undertake work of this nature. Your specialised training warrants it, however, and I do not think you will mind the obvious danger attached to the task.

'The only other thing I would impress on you is that the radio station we are endeavouring to locate is not a static one. It has been picked up in slightly different places at different times, so it seems likely that the operator is in the habit of moving it about to minimise the possibility of being spotted and discovered.'

Brandon nodded in understanding. He had guessed that would be the case already. 'May we know what manner of messages are being passed by code between this foreign power and the secret radio in the jungle?' he asked.

The V.I.P. hesitated for an instant. Then: 'We were able to break the code at one point during the transmissions,' he replied. 'Naturally they continually change it, but the small amount of information we gained from one message led us to believe that an uprising among the native tribes is by no means as remote a possibility as lots of people like to think. That, I regret to say, is all I can tell you. However, do not imagine for a moment that we are making too great a thing of this. It is really serious, and unless it is stopped, and stopped quickly, we shall have something taking shape in our midst that will be as ugly as any revolution the world has ever known or experienced.'

Brandon thought of the man with the red beard out in the jungle. He remembered what the pigmy chief had told him. He thought of a number of tiny pointers and stored them away in his brain. At the moment the connection between a man who could tame the gorillas and make them do his bidding and a man who worked a secret radio station seemed hopelessly fantastic. But Brandon knew as well as anyone that even more fantastic things had and would happen in the untold depths of the vast African continent.

'Thank you, sir,' he murmured. 'You've been very helpful.'

The big man inclined his head graciously. 'Graham will fit you up with maps and bearings to take you as close as is known to the latest location point we have,' he said. He rose from his chair, placing his hands flat on the surface of the table. 'And now, gentlemen, I think we can call this meeting to a close. You, Brandon, and you, McNulty, will certainly want a decent rest tonight if you are setting off in the morning. I will not detain you any longer.'

There was a general clatter of chairs being thrust back from the table. Men talked in hushed whispers, many of them glancing at Brandon and his companion. The little sandy-haired Scot seemed perfectly at ease as he sauntered across and helped himself to a long drink of whisky and soda from the sideboard table at the far end of the room.

Brandon found himself beside Graham, the R.A.F. man, who grinned and twirled the ends of his enormous moustache confidently. 'Jolly good show, what?' he murmured. 'I hope you won't resent it, old man, but I'm coming with you tomorrow. Sort of liaison, you know. Grand show, I call it.'

Brandon blinked a little. There was

something very likable about Graham, but he had not expected to have him as a companion on safari. He wondered if the man would stand up to the strain of continued jungle movement. However, that remained to be seen.

By now, general conversation had broken out in the room. McNulty was chatting to another man about geology. Given a fair chance, McNulty would talk of nothing else, provided he could get an audience patient enough to listen to the innumerable stories he fitted into his text.

Brandon grinned at Graham. 'There are one or two things you and I could usefully discuss,' he said quietly.

'Bang on, old boy!' came the answer. 'This jungle life fascinates me, you know! Heard of a fella once who pranged his kite right in the middle of the Congo. Lord knows how he managed it, Brandon, but the poor devil walked — *walked*, mind you! — near on a thousand miles before he landed up at a village. Pretty well all in by then, he was. They gave him the D.F.C., among other things. Wizard show!'

Brandon hid a smile, keeping his face straight with difficulty. 'Speaking of aeroplanes,' he murmured, 'I had an odd story told me by a pigmy chief a few days ago.'

'You don't say? Let's have it!' The moustache was twitching excitedly in spite of Graham's efforts to cling to its ends with his fingers. He helped himself to a long drink with shining eyes.

'Yes,' said Brandon grimly. 'I came across a queer customer in the jungle. Fellow who used a tame gorilla as a guard and sentry. He lives in a hut in a tree — the man, I mean. That darned gorilla near enough had me.'

Graham blinked. 'Wizard show!' he breathed. 'You killed it of course?'

Brandon nodded. 'It was the creature's master that intrigued me more than the animal itself, though,' he added. 'Tall red-haired man with a beard. Foreigner of some sort. You've never heard yarns about him, have you?'

Graham shook his head sadly. 'Gorilla tamer, eh?' he mused. 'Reminds me of a wallah I once saw in a circus. Old man

75

who could do simply anything with animals! Simply anything. Amazin', that's what it is! Have another drink?'

'Thanks,' replied Brandon automatically. He hardly knew what he was doing as he took the proffered glass. He knew now what had struck him about the bearded man's general appearance. It *had* been recognition, all right. Years before, Brandon had seen the man, but under entirely different circumstances, in different clothes and different surroundings, with different animals, and without a beard. His uncanny memory for faces had not deceived him. The bearded man in the Congo jungle had been a lion tamer in a circus he'd seen several years previously on one of his rare visits to London. The realisation was staggering, but he could not blink his eyes at the facts. He knew they were true despite the apparent absurdity of it.

For a moment he did not quite know what to do about the knowledge he had gained. It should be checked before he acted on it or reported what he suspected. With a word to Graham, he excused himself and made his way to the radio room.

There he wrote out a cable for transmission to London. Among Brandon's many acquaintances and friends he numbered all manner of people. The one to whom he sent his cable was a showbusiness agent.

He knew he could not expect to receive a reply before he left in the morning. In fact he doubted if the agent would have the information he needed for several days, but at least he had set the wheels in motion and could await results. It was only a matter of confirmation, in any case. By the time he returned from the coming journey, his message would either have established certain facts or denounced them as wrong.

Returning to Graham, he forced himself to chat amiably about nothing in particular, leaving the initiative with the R.A.F. man. Graham enjoyed himself, telling stories and talking of this and that with a freedom from care that almost made Brandon envious of the man.

Presently McNulty sidled up to them. Brandon was thinking of turning in, and the arrival of the Scot gave him an excuse to break off his conversation with

Graham. McNulty said: 'I've been hearing all about this film lass ye've lost. Seems a mighty bad shame that a wee gal should be lost in this terrible jungle!'

Brandon nodded soberly. 'Glory Fanshawe, wasn't it?' he put in. 'I saw her in a film once. Pretty kid.'

'Absolutely wizard little thing,' said Graham sadly.

'How did she get lost?' asked Brandon. 'Haven't they found her yet?'

'Hopeless, old fellow! It was this way. She and her co-star went out on a short hunting trip. They'd been working on location not so far from here, you know. Well, the man — can't stand him at any price — came back alone in a dreadful state. Something had scared poor Glory so badly that she had run for her life. He'd gone after her, fallen into a swamp because he didn't look where he was going, and lost her completely.'

'Haven't they sent out search parties?'

'Oh Lord, yes! Dozens of 'em. Put up a wizard show and all that, but they never found her. She's probably dead by this time.' He stared into his glass dejectedly, twisting one end of his moustache with sudden violence.

Brandon frowned. 'Too bad,' he commented dryly. 'Whereabouts did all this happen? Remember, I've been out of touch for several weeks.'

Graham glanced round mysteriously. 'Not far from where we're going,' he whispered. 'Never know, we might even find her body ourselves!'

6

The Death Canoe

Brandon and McNulty were allotted a
bungalow near the radio station. Impo
and Muuma arrived to look after their
employers, bringing the news that everything was ready for an early start in the
morning. What stores were required had
all been laid on by the station authorities:
a couple of efficient Belgian officials, plump
and cheerful in spite of the sudden influx
of notable company that had descended
on them with little or no warning.

Brandon said practically nothing while
McNulty and he were undressing. The air
was stifling, and tiredness was heavy on
the shoulders of both men. They bade
each other goodnight. Brandon turned off
the light and closed his eyes with a sigh of
relief. The evening had been a greater
strain than he had imagined. In the
manner of all men accustomed to living

in the wilds, he was soon fast asleep; nor did anything disturb his rest till Impo arrived before dawn with cups of steaming tea.

It was still dark when they breakfasted. Graham came and joined them with the news that the 'old man', as he called the V.I.P., had been very impressed by the manner and readiness with which they had accepted the assignment. There would be rich recognition if the trip proved successful. The idea of going with them himself had been his own, and had also met with approval when he mooted it. Now he was as enthusiastic as Brandon himself, and as eager to be away.

McNulty was bubbling over as they breakfasted. His mercurial temperament could hardly wait to be on the trail once again, and the prospect of avoiding a dry discussion with the mineralogical authorities regarding the samples he had brought back with him was shelved for the time being.

The sun had barely lifted above the rim of the distant hills before they were off, heading back towards the green hell of jungle terrain through which Brandon and McNulty had struggled during previous weeks.

'We'll do better to stick to the bank of the Tongwi River for a time,' said Brandon. 'Country's less dense there, and going upstream it leads almost straight to the district we want.'

Graham was ready enough to fall in with the plan. He had travelled the jungle before, but was not, of course, as experienced a man as his two companions.

The Tongwi flowed between walls of undergrowth, barred here and there by mud flats and tumbling rapids according to the nature of its immediate surroundings. Eventually it would empty itself into the mighty Congo, to swell the waters of one of the biggest rivers in the world. The country was alive with game of every sort, and in spite of the gravity of their mission all three men did a fair amount of shooting during the first day out. It was not until around noon on the second day that they came across anything that could be connected in any way with the object of their search.

Struggling through tangled lianas and thorn scrub, they were heading the long file of bearers, hacking a path through the undergrowth with keen-bladed machetes. The heat was terrific, so that sweat poured down their faces and necks in a constant stream. Even Brandon and McNulty were feeling the effects of the torrid heat, while Graham suffered agonies but refused to show it. There was tougher fibre in the man than Brandon had dared to hope, and his brief acquaintance with him made him glad that Graham had joined them.

On one hand flowed the stream of the Tongwi; on the other was the chattering, noisy world of the jungle. One of them was constantly on the alert with a rifle as they fought on through the scrub and trees, for this was no place to be taken unawares by a charging beast of the wilds.

Graham paused and wiped his face with the once-clean sleeve of his shirt. 'Lord, but it's hot!' he sighed. Some of the drawling laziness had gone from his voice since the party had left Ruchuru, but his amiable grin was as much in evidence as ever.

'Keeps the fat down, doesn't it?' said Brandon, meeting his gaze. 'McNulty's the lucky one. He's so small he can't be shrivelled up much more than he is already!'

McNulty glared at them both as they laughed. 'Dinna ye think I'm so lucky!' he snapped. 'Bein' thin as I am, the sun goes through me an' out the other side. Mon, but I'm fried alive in this place!' He brandished his fly whisk viciously and stamped on through the bush.

Suddenly Graham, who was walking beside Brandon as they hacked and smashed their way along, came to an abrupt halt. Brandon sensed that his eyes had seen something of interest. 'Hang on, Mac!' he said softly.

McNulty stopped at once, freezing where he was. There was a note of urgency in Brandon's voice that warned him to silence.

Brandon followed Graham's pointing finger. The man was peering intently upstream from where they stood among the scrub on the banks of the river. 'Canoe,' he muttered. 'Coming this way.'

Brandon eased his rifle from his shoulder and slid back the safety catch. Even a dugout canoe could be dangerous in the Congo country. A man never knew what to expect. He raised his hand to Impo, close behind him. Impo sent a whispered order back and halted the line of bearers. The canoe drifted silently nearer.

'No one in it,' muttered Graham disgustedly. 'We're gettin' the jitters over nothing! Bang on, fellows!'

But Brandon shook his head. His lips were tight as he stared at the oncoming canoe. Something grey and dirty was humped in the bottom of it. He could just see the top of whatever it was. 'Not so fast,' he breathed. 'It isn't empty.'

Graham shaded his eyes again. Then he whistled softly. 'You're right!' he agreed. 'It's a man!'

The canoe was very much closer to them by this time. They could all see what it held now. Hunched in the shallow dugout log was a crumpled figure, face down, still.

Brandon was at once alive. Impo,

standing close to his back, stepped forward quickly. 'I will go look, *bwana*,' he murmured.

'Fine — I'll cover you from crocs. Hurry, Impo!'

Impo needed no second word. He darted through the thin screen of thorn bush between the narrow path and the water's edge. A moment later they were watching as he splashed his way into the shallow water and grabbed hold of the canoe with one hand, turning it towards the bank. The timing had been perfect, for the current at this point was fairly swift.

Ready hands grasped the canoe and drew it close to the bank. McNulty swore quietly as he stared downwards at its burden. Brandon's mouth hardened grimly. Graham said nothing, but hauled the boat half out of the water. All the lazy humour was gone from his features as he glanced up at Brandon. 'Let's get him out,' he said curtly.

McNulty stopped swearing. The three of them bent and lifted the inert body of the man from the bottom of the canoe. They did it with a natural gentleness, carrying him back to the jungle pathway and lowering him carefully to the ground. Then McNulty and Graham stood back while Brandon knelt beside the body.

He saw the prematurely aged face of a youngish man, tanned to the colour of mahogany by exposure. Once it had been a handsome, cavalier face. Now it was swollen and distorted by unshielded heat and sores. A long, jagged wound ran the length of the forehead. The wound was thick with crawling flies.

Brandon stared downwards grimly. His hand went out and lifted the limp wrist of the man. With a surprisingly delicate touch, his fingers sought for a pulse. He did not expect to find one, and was completely amazed when the faint flutter communicated itself to his sensitive fingertips. 'He's alive!' he hissed softly. 'Brandy, quickly!'

Graham fished a flask from his hip pocket and un-stoppered it hurriedly, kneeling beside Brandon. Brandon took the flask and let a little of the spirit dribble into the senseless man's mouth, holding his lower lip down with a finger as he did so. For several seconds nothing happened, then the man gave an unmistakable cough and gasped for breath in a spasm.

Brandon cradled his head, waiting anxiously. Had they been in time to learn anything from this dying wreck? He had an instinctive intuition that the man had something to do with their own immediate mission. There was nothing solid to explain the feeling, but Brandon knew it was so. He had come to rely on these hunches in the past, and they had rarely let him down or proved themselves false.

'Is he coming round?' queried Graham.

'Don't know yet,' was the answer.

'Och, but the poor wee laddie's in a mighty bad way,' grunted McNulty soberly. 'See, mon, he's been stabbed in the side, and his wrists are all cut with ropes. Been a prisoner of some devil!'

'Yes.' Brandon's voice was flat.

The man on the ground stirred slightly, then his eyes flickered open for a moment before closing again. He moved his lips in a helpless fashion. There was something pitiful in the sight. Brandon gave him a little more brandy. With the curious eyes of the bearers watching them, the three men waited.

Again the dying man opened his eyes, glazed and dim. The shadow of Brandon covered him. His lips moved slowly and painfully as he stared unseeingly upwards. 'Machine guns,' he whispered. 'Hundreds of guns and bombs. Tell them about it; warn them. You're all in danger.' The disjointed, stumbling words faded out.

'Take it easy,' said Brandon gently. He had to bend his ear close to the man's mouth to hear what he said at all. It was obvious that his life was limited to minutes now. There was nothing they could do about it. He was so close to death as to be beyond help.

'Where will the danger come from?' asked Graham. 'Tell us that, old boy. For God's sake, tell us more.'

The dying man opened his eyes again. His head lolled sideways, but he managed to straighten it up for a moment. 'The native fury,' he whispered. 'Upstream. There's a white woman there, too. Save her if you can, but get word back of what

I say. Native fury. It'll sweep the land if it starts.'

'Native fury?' echoed Brandon slowly.

'The natives. Guns and bombs and machine guns . . . You must stop it. There may not be a lot of time . . . '

'Who's leading this danger?'

But the man on the ground was silent. Great spouts of blood flowed from the corner of his mouth now. His eyes were closed, and his breathing, which before had been weak, was now gusty and rattling. The end was coming swiftly. Brandon and McNulty exchanged glances. There was nothing more to learn. Before he could speak again, the man on the ground gave a final choking gasp. His body went stiff, arching upwards for an instant; then it was limp and dead.

'He's gone, poor devil,' muttered Graham.

Brandon knelt where he was for fully thirty seconds, staring down at the tortured face of the dead man. His thoughts were grim, but were now resolving into a number of clear convictions.

'See if the laddie's got anything on, him,' said McNulty. 'I canna see what we can do but bury him now.'

Graham nodded. 'Who the devil is he anyway?' he said.

Brandon shook his head. 'I wouldn't know,' he replied. He felt in the man's stained and torn bush shirt. There was a dirty singlet beneath it. His shorts were in rags, and the soles of his heavy boots were worn right through. Searching through the clothes, Brandon felt a bulge in one of the pockets of the shirt. He pulled out a crumpled blue handkerchief.

'Something,' he said grimly. 'This is all there is.' He spread the handkerchief on the ground. It was stained with blood.

'It's a woman's!' grunted Graham in surprise. 'Look, Rex, there's something embroidered in the corner.'

'G and F, with a lot of frilly knots and things,' mused Brandon. 'Now . . . '

'The lad said something about a woman,' put in McNulty. 'It's probably hers. G.F.'

'Good Lord, the Fanshawe woman!' said Graham, a great light dawning on him.

'Of course,' said Brandon. 'We're all a

bit slow in the uptake, aren't we?' He pulled a rueful face. 'Do you know, I'd forgotten all about her! It looks as if she's entangled in this affair, too. If this chap escaped, he must have left her behind. Wish I knew who he was.'

Graham snapped his fingers suddenly. 'I'll tell you who he is!' he said explosively.

They stared at him.

'He's the U.N. agent who's been on the job. Grainger! We'll have to send word back to base the moment we can!'

Brandon nodded. He felt he was being extraordinarily dull just lately. The whole thing should have been plain to him. It must be the heat and the fact that his thoughts had been busy with other angles, he decided. 'Impo,' he called.

'Yes, sir?'

'Set the transmitter up at once. We'll stop where we are for an hour or so. Have some of the other men dig a grave.'

Impo nodded gloomily. 'Yes, *bwana*.'

While the activity was going on, Brandon and the others discussed the situation. Brandon voiced his ideas about the red-bearded man in the jungle having had some hand in the business. At first McNulty and Graham did not know what to make of it, but in the end they came to thinking as he did. The coincidence, and the facts that supported it, were too strong to ignore.

In touch with Ruchuru by radio, Brandon handed over to Graham. There was a lengthy conversation, at the end of which Graham explained the outcome. 'It was Grainger, all right,' he said grimly. 'I gave headquarters a description of him. They say we must follow up where he left off.' He clenched his fist tightly and stared at the ground. 'We've got to kill or capture the man responsible for what he called The Fury. The latest news makes it certain that someone, some foreign power, is working stealthily to cause disruption among the natives in this part of Africa. From what I can gather, there's a danger that arms will be supplied when the time comes for a general rising. It's serious and has got to be stopped.

'We're the only people in the probable vicinity of the root of operations. This is tied in with the secret radio, of course, and it's definitely our pigeon. Other forces will follow us up, but we've got to strike!' He broke off and grinned in a boyish manner. 'Wizard show, what?'

'Aye, it may be,' answered McNulty somewhat sourly. 'If that's the case, we'd best be moving.'

The radio was closed down and packed away. The body of Grainger was buried. Brandon said a few words over the grave, while McNulty whittled a cross and hammered it into the earth mound at the dead man's head. 'Weel,' he said quietly, 'they say that an agent must get his news through no matter what happens, but Grainger was a lucky man to live long enough to meet up with us. We've a lot to be thankful for, and I ken that the laddie should rest at ease now.'

The three men stood with bared heads for a minute or two. Then Brandon squared his broad shoulders. 'Come on,' he said grimly. 'I'll level with the man who did this if I have to chase him across the earth!'

Graham shot him a glance. 'You can count me in on that show,' he added.

'Aye, and me too,' said McNulty. 'Let's be going.'

They followed the line of the river for the rest of that day, coming at evening to a vast mangrove swamp. It spread out in front of them, completely barring further passage.

Brandon halted and scowled. His eyes sought the far bank of the river in a speculative fashion. There was scrub over there, which spoke of solid ground. 'We'd be wise to cross and carry on over there,' he said.

They followed his gaze. The river was broad; here and there its surface was disturbed by underwater movement. The ugly snouts of crocodiles showed and disappeared in large numbers as they watched.

'We can build a raft,' said McNulty. 'It won't take so verra long, and we'd save ourselves miles an' miles of goin' round this stuff.'

Brandon nodded. Graham left the decision to his two companions; he was willing to fall in with any plan they considered best.

McNulty shouted to Muuma. Brandon

called Impo. The two headmen stood waiting while the position was explained. Before many minutes were up, the scene was one of intense activity.

'There'll just be time to get the raft made before dark, Mac,' said Brandon. 'We can ferry across at dawn. I wouldn't want to risk it tonight.'

'Aye, I was just thinkin' the same, lad. That stream is alive with crocs, the ugly devils!'

The work went on apace, so that just as the swift darkness fell the raft was completed. In the meantime, camp had been made by some of the bearers and everything was set for the night. The leaders divided the hours into watches, for it was plain that they were now in what Graham termed 'enemy country'. Noise was kept to a minimum, and they all agreed that no guns should be fired except in a case of emergency.

The night passed uneventfully. Before dawn the camp was astir. No fires were allowed by Brandon, so that the morning meal was makeshift in the extreme. However, they promised themselves better fare when they reached a less vulnerable position — or completed their mission, which ever came first.

Drinking cold coffee from a flask, Brandon looked at the Scotsman. 'You'd better get your men over first,' he said. 'And take Graham with you, Mac. I'll wait here. Impo can cross with you and take a couple of my men to bring the raft back. It won't hold all of us at once anyway. How'll that suit you?'

They nodded agreement. The raft was already being loaded with stores and equipment. Brandon talked with Impo and full arrangements were made. Then the first party set off, poling their way over the crocodile-infested stretch of water. There was a certain amount of risk, but not enough to deter them, and the splashing of the poles kept any venturesome crocs at a distance. Brandon watched from the edge of the mangrove swamp, the dark tangle of monstrous growth at his back. With him were six of his men, the rest having found ample room to cross with McNulty and Graham.

Slowly the raft returned, with Impo

and his two fellows. Brandon glanced round as the raft grounded on the mud. Everything was still and quiet; only the scurrying life of the jungle stirred. He stepped onto the raft, rifle slung from his shoulder. Impo grinned and plunged his pole into the mud, thrusting off with it. The other two men did the same. Very slowly the cumbersome vessel slid out towards the centre of the stream.

It was still closer to the mangrove growth than the far bank when Brandon looked back. Then several things happened at the same time.

Brandon caught a glimpse of blue steel flashing for an instant in the sunlight. He yelled an instinctive warning, dropping flat as he did so, snaking his rifle to his shoulder. Hardly had the words left his mouth before there was another sudden flash and a flat report. The whistle of a bullet passed close to his head. It missed him but struck one of the bearers in the stomach, doubling him up in screaming agony.

Brandon got his finger on the trigger and sighted on the spot from which the treacherous shot had come. Before he could fire, however, the raft gave a violent lurch, tipping sideways. Impo shouted in alarm. The other men were thrown into the water with a splash; then Brandon himself was floundering in the warm, brackish flood.

With all his immediate thoughts on saving his life, he heard the unmistakable scream of a woman from the mangroves.

7

Combat!

It all happened so quickly that for once in his life Rex Brandon was taken unawares. He had not expected to be fired on by an unseen marksman; he had not expected the raft to be overturned by the surprised wallowing of a giant river horse or hippo; and the last thing he had expected to hear was the terrified scream of a woman — though he knew that a woman was somewhere in the green hell of jungle that spread for miles and miles in all directions.

Coming on top of one another in such swift succession, the combination of events left him gasping for breath and striking out for his life in the croc-infested water. The nearer bank was the obvious place to make for, and the fact that there was a concealed rifleman waiting for him did not deter him. He knew quite well that he would probably be attacked by crocodiles long before he could reach the other shore, where Graham and McNulty were waiting in an agony of suspense. His choice was the lesser of two evils.

He had lost his rifle, but still retained his revolver. A glance over his shoulder in the troubled water showed him that Impo had survived and was swimming strongly beside him. Of the other men there was no sign, one being dead and the others dragged down by the ever-ravenous crocs.

'Keep going, Impo!' Brandon shouted. 'We'll make it!'

'Yes, *bwana*,' gasped Impo. There was a subtle lack of conviction in his voice.

Thrashing violently with their arms and legs, the two of them struggled towards the bank. Brandon expected to hear the vicious whiplash-crack of a rifle at any moment, but it did not come. Instead he was suddenly confronted with the gaping jaws of one of the biggest crocodiles he had ever seen.

Treading water to keep himself afloat, he reached down for his revolver. Just as he wrenched it free, the jaws of the croc snapped shut within an inch of his arm. The great creature surged forward like a torpedo. At the same moment there was a crashing report from the opposite bank. A miniature fountain of water spurted up alongside the crocodile as a bullet whipped out from McNulty's rifle. The Scot yelled encouragement. Impo screamed another warning and flailed out with his arms and legs as a second croc bored in to the attack.

Once more a rifle spat from the opposite bank. There was a dull thud as the bullet smashed into the giant croc's body; but the impact only seemed to infuriate it. Brandon found himself struggling to keep clear of the slashing jaws as he turned and twisted to get a close shot at the beast. Long claws ripped at his leg as the saurian rolled like a porpoise. He seized the opportunity and thrust his gun almost into the creature's mouth, pulling the trigger as he did so.

The concussion jarred the length of his arm. A moment later the water was stained with a scarlet gush from the crocodile's throat. It rolled away, the thick length of its tail slashing like an armoured flail. The tip of it struck Impo across the back, tearing the skin off his flesh and bringing a scream to his lips. He gave a strangled gasp and sank out of sight. Brandon cursed savagely. The giant crocodile was dead, floating belly-up. Another was coming towards them fast, rows of teeth gleaming yellow in the morning light. Brandon's revolver crashed again, the bullet tearing straight between the creature's teeth and ripping upwards to its brain.

Then Brandon glanced round anxiously. He knew he could not expect much assistance from McNulty and Graham. Without a boat they could not reach him, and the raft was floating downstream sluggishly, twisting and turning slowly in the current.

Impo broke the surface, gurgling for breath and thrashing at the water. Brandon thrust his revolver into its holster and grabbed the man round the shoulders. With powerful strokes of his legs he drove towards the bank, dragging Impo with him. Then there was soft glutinous mud under his feet and the water gave less support. He looked round a little desperately, wondering what had happened to the unseen man with the rifle. And what had become of the woman who had cried out in terror from the mangroves?

But there was no time for speculation. Impo was in a bad way, for the crocodile's tail had left an ugly wound in his flesh. Brandon knelt on the ground beside him. Impo gazed up at him, eyes rolling horridly.

'You go, *bwana*,' he said. 'Leave me. Find the man with the rifle.'

Brandon glanced round. He stood up and called across to McNulty and Graham. Some of the bearers were running downstream in the wake of the drifting raft. It would be some considerable time before they overtook it and succeeded in bringing it to the bank.

McNulty said: 'Sit tight, Rex. We'll come across as soon as we can, laddie. How's Impo?'

'He'll make out all right,' shouted Brandon. 'See you later.'

Before the others could say anything further, he turned to Impo. 'Stay where you are till they come to fetch you, Impo,' he said. 'I'm going after the man with the rifle.'

'Yes, sir. Kill him if you can! He must be a very bad *mulungu*!'

'A powerful juju man,' muttered Brandon to himself. 'Red-bearded devil, more likely!'

He struck off through the tangled forest of mangrove, casting round in the soft earth for prints that would put him on the track of the unseen marksman. Starting at the approximate place from which the shot had come, he soon found what he was after. The prints of a barefooted man showed plainly on the ground. The man had been running, as if he had suddenly taken to his heels after firing upon the raft.

The explanation was not far to seek. A second set of prints, much smaller and lighter than the first man's, came to view as Brandon quartered the ground nearby. The woman of course, he decided. She'd screamed, perhaps in warning, perhaps in fear when Red Beard caught sight of her and gave chase. Brandon did not know the correct answer to his queries, but somewhere ahead of him in the jungle of treacherous mangrove growth was the man he sought.

In the distance he could hear McNulty and Graham shouting to the men as they did their best to reassemble the party before crossing the river again to their companion's aid. Brandon smiled grimly to himself. It seemed as if he was engaged on one of those lone commando assignments. A pity he had lost his rifle in the river. If he did come face to face with the bearded man, he would be at a serious disadvantage armed only with his revolver.

The track was leading him deeper and deeper into the dense wet jungle of mangrove. The ground underfoot was so soft as to be more like mud than earth, but it still held sufficient solidity to show up the footprints of the man he followed. Then he realised that the prints of the woman were no longer visible. She must have given her pursuer the slip at some point, unless he had overtaken her and was carrying her bodily with him. He was a powerful enough man to do it, thought

Brandon, but somehow or other he did not think that was the solution.

Pushing on, he paused to listen. There was an eerie stillness in the mangrove swamp. Only the soft gurgling of the moist earth amid the millions of roots gave forth any sound. This place seemed devoid of animal life; there was not even birdsong to break the silence.

Then Brandon caught the sound of shouting and yelling from a distance. He reckoned the din was coming from the other bank of the river, where Graham and McNulty had been. Had something else happened to them? It was a worrying thought, but he kept on regardless, knowing that McNulty at any rate was well able to take care of himself and the men. Nor was Graham a fool.

The echoing crack of a distant shot was added to the general noise. It was followed almost immediately by a second report, duller and heavier: the crash of a revolver. Brandon tightened his mouth, wondering if he ought to have remained on the riverbank instead of blundering off on a trail of his own. It was difficult to say at the moment; he had been driven by an instinctive urge to speed when he set off alone. Now the others might be needing him. But still he pushed on alone.

Without warning, the mangroves thinned out to a flat expanse of bare ground. It was roughly circular in shape, about fifty yards across: a kind of island in the tangle of gnarled mangroves; a lake of soil in a quagmire of shaky mud. Brandon halted abruptly, peering ahead, expecting to see some sign of the man he trailed. But the footprints led straight across the clearing, to disappear on the far side on a course parallel with the line of the river some quarter of a mile away. Gripping his revolver ready for an instant shot, Brandon started across the clearing with the caution of a leopard stalking its prey. He knew that he should have circled the clearing, for now he had no cover whatever; but he still felt that speed was essential.

The opposite side of the clearing was reached without mishap. With one eye on the undergrowth and the other on the tracks of the man he sought, Brandon thrust his way into the close world of the mangroves once more. They barred his way and snagged at his clothes, but he forced himself through them. After something like a hundred yards of this tedious progress, another clearing opened in front of him. This one was nothing but a narrow strip across which he must make his way. Glancing up and down its length, he darted over, plunging into the mangroves again, thankful for the cover they offered.

Then the ground became softer than ever, showing pools of stagnant water here and there that sucked at his boots as he splashed along. The ground was giving way to swamp. He wondered how much further the red-bearded man would penetrate it. He was not afraid of sinking in the morass, because where the man had gone he could go also; and the footprints were still acting as his guide.

Presently the tracks changed direction sharply, taking a turn towards the river bank again. Brandon followed them grimly. He knew that the man ahead could not have such a very big start on him. He could, in fact, be lying in wait a few yards away, for it was impossible to see far in the denseness that hemmed him in. Brandon accepted the risk.

Then suddenly he lost the line of prints altogether. The ground had softened to such an extent that they were no longer visible. Mud and water had swamped them over, smoothing them out. Brandon halted, swearing softly as he stared round with an uneasy sense of defeat.

It was while he was standing there that a sound behind his back brought him round sharply. He levelled his revolver for a shot.

Pushing through the mangroves were a number of gorillas. Brandon froze where he was, eyes darting this way and that. The monstrous creatures seemed to be coming towards him from all sides. There was only one direction in which he could go: the way he had been following the bearded man.

He held his fire and began to retreat cautiously, not wanting to force the gorillas to attack until he could see some way of outdistancing them. If only he could reach a stretch of clear ground, he thought desperately. In this tangled stuff they would be able to overtake him in a matter of yards. Their powerful bodies would act as tanks to smash a way through.

Still the line of gorillas continued to converge on him. He counted something like a score of the brutes, some big, some younger and smaller. One of them, a mighty old bull, beat its chest in a thunderous tattoo and let out a squealing bellow of rage as it advanced.

Brandon went on backing cautiously away, glancing over his shoulder every now and again.

The man and the gorillas must have covered nearly fifty yards in this manner when Brandon saw what he had been praying for. Behind him now was a small clearing, flat and solid underfoot. Breaking from the mangroves, he turned and raced across it. Behind him the enormous apes let out a shrill chorus of anger as they shambled in his wake. A quick glance showed the man that they were not far behind. Had he wanted any further proof that his enemy was the bearded man, it was there in the herd of gorillas, for they were plainly attacking him on orders of some sort.

He was almost across the clearing by now, his feet thudding dully on the soft ground. Then with a startled exclamation he stopped, whirling to face the oncoming apes. The ground had changed swiftly. He had only just saved himself from plunging headlong into a bright green morass that barred his way. It lay in a broad ribbon, separating him from the refuge of the dense mangroves on the other side.

The security of the clearing for which he had prayed, and the speed he had been able to make in crossing it, disappeared in a second. He was trapped within yards of a ravening herd of savage animals. Behind him was a swamp, a deadly strip of bright green slime and death. In front were the apes, their slavering jaws and yellow fangs eager to seize him, their long arms and broad, thick hands ready to tear him limb from limb.

Brandon knew the chances were pretty thin. With only a revolver against a score of such beasts, he would be lucky indeed to come out of this alive. But he determined to sell his life as dearly as possible for all that.

Crouching down, he brought his revolver up, steadied it and fired at the nearest of the swiftly approaching gorillas. The fight was on, but even Rex Brandon would not bet on his chances of survival.

8

Disappearing Woman

Brandon's first shot brought the enormous leader of the apes toppling forward on the ground, its great paws clawing at its stomach where the heavy lead bullet had thudded home. The rest of the animals paused for an instant, but the groans of their leader urged them on to do battle. With fierce cries and grunts of rage, they came pounding towards Brandon. He fired again, bringing another of the brutes to its knees. With three more shots he wounded another and killed two more. But there was only one more shot left in the revolver and no time to reload.

The gorillas were close now; so close that he could almost smell their fetid breath as they pressed in on him. And retreat meant certain death in the green morass of slime at his back. And there were still over a dozen of the savage apes to deal with.

Brandon crouched on the edge of the swamp, muscles bunched for a spring this way or that according to which direction the next assault would take. The gorillas gave him a momentary respite, grouping together a few yards away as if preparing for a final rush. He knew that if they did that it would be all up; he would be overwhelmed in a moment. Then he noticed that several of the creatures were sniffing the air suspiciously.

He began to edge his way further along the brink of the swamp, feeling for more cartridges as he did so. But one of the nearer of the gorillas suddenly grunted and lunged forward. Its hairy paw smashed down on Brandon's wrist, nearly breaking it. The revolver went spinning from his grasp as he darted back out of reach. His hand whipped round and grasped his hunting-knife, dragging it from its sheath with feverish haste. The other gorillas stood and watched their companion as it shuffled towards Brandon again, grunting and reaching out with its great thick arms.

Brandon aimed carefully and stabbed

forwards with the knife. He remembered having done the same thing not so long back. Would the outcome of this fight be as lucky for him as the last time? The odds were so great that he doubted it.

The keen-edged blade of the knife buried itself to the hilt in the flesh of the animal's forearm, causing it to scream in mingled rage and pain. Brandon whirled aside from the flailing blow that was aimed at his head. His foot sank to the knee in the slime at his back. Only with the greatest difficulty did he save himself. And the gorilla was almost on top of him!

Then, just as he thought the beast would seize him and finish the fight, one of the other apes uttered a weird cry that echoed back and forth among the mangroves on the other side of the clearing. As if the cry had some special meaning, the remainder of the creatures whirled round clumsily, most of them facing the clearing. Only the one who was bent on attacking Brandon remained facing the swamp. With a sudden squealing cry it launched itself again. Brandon, by the quickest movement he had ever made in his life before, escaped the violence of the assault, sidestepping in the nick of time. With a fearful cry, the gorilla lumbered past him. Then it struck the quaking surface of the morass in a spray of mud and slime. Within a second it had disappeared from view, sucked down and suffocated by the treacherous bright green strip.

Brandon heaved a sigh that was half relief, half renewed determination. He turned to face his enemies once more. They seemed to be hesitating, some staring uncertainly at the dark wall of the mangrove jungle. But the rest were still watching Brandon, some even shambling closer and closer to him. He gritted his teeth and began to edge forwards to meet the nearest. Maybe the same thing would happen when it charged. If he could account for any more of the brutes without harm to himself, all the better.

But the expected charge never came. Instead there was a repetition of the shrill cry of warning from one of the apes. At the same instant the edge of the jungle was violently disturbed by some swiftly moving shape. Then a tawny-haired beast erupted into view, the sunlight slanting down on its spotted coat. It stood there, a fine example of a leopard, snarling and baring its fangs as it studied the herd of gorillas with yellow, malignant eyes.

Brandon thanked heaven in a silent breath of words. The gorillas were immediately thrown into confusion, turning this way and that in the face of fresh danger and a foe whose potential they knew of old.

The leopard launched itself across the clearing, making straight for the biggest of the gorillas. Brandon knew that unless he seized this chance it would be his last day on earth. He himself went in to the attack. The leopard, a furry shape of lithe, spitting fury, hurtled through the air, landing on the gorilla's chest and bearing it backwards. More of the gorillas gathered round, some trying to tear the leopard off their companion, others starting to make off in the direction of the jungle at a shambling run.

Then Rex Brandon was among them himself, slashing and stabbing with his knife. The air was hideous with the screams and snarls of the fighting ape and its deadly enemy. Other cries were added to the turmoil as Brandon wrought havoc with his knife. But his luck did not last for as long as he would have liked it to. His object had been to carve a way through the herd to freedom. Everything would have been all right had not one of the apes succeeded in striking the knife from his grip as he thrust with the blade. Unarmed, he was suddenly at a hopeless disadvantage. There was no clear way to run for escape, though the mortal combat going on between the leopard and the gorilla had eased the situation considerably. Only about half the apes now threatened his life, but that was quite sufficient under the circumstances.

The gorilla that had dashed the knife from his hand now lowered his head and rushed at him. Brandon stood still as a rock, waiting. His knife and his revolver were both well out of reach. Tensing himself, he prepared for the final battle that was being thrust upon him. Already weary with the strain of his previous exertions, he met the gorilla as best he could, grabbing at its arms and wrenching them down. The creature's foul breath fanned his face as he bent over backwards to avoid the drooling fangs. Then he was making the most desperate effort of his whole career. The muscles of his back strained and creaked as he put all his strength into the hand-to-hand fight for his life. Only by a supreme show of muscular power did he keep the gorilla from rending him limb from limb. He used his feet as well as his hands and arms, crushing down on the brute's great toes mercilessly. The gorilla squealed in fury. Brandon gritted his teeth as he heaved and struggled for mastery. Very slowly his strength was telling. But the strain was so great that he knew he could not keep it up. Already wounded by the knife, the mighty ape was not as powerful as it might have been. But Brandon himself was weakening. He had to finish the fight quickly or lose it for good.

With one last tremendous wrench, he lifted the gorilla clean off the ground, holding the kicking, squirming beast above his head. Though it shrieked its rage, it was almost helpless, beating at the air. Brandon turned slowly to face the remainder of the apes. He saw that the leopard had overcome the one it had attacked. There was a snarling shape tearing at the hot flesh. Some more of the gorillas had taken flight, leaving less than a dozen to threaten Brandon.

With sweat pouring down his face and into his eyes, he staggered towards them. Then he halted as they began to shamble forwards. Calling on all his reserves for one last exertion that almost broke his back, he hurled the body of the gorilla full in their faces, turning to run as its weight left his arms.

Darting along the very edge of the swamp, he managed to avoid the squealing pursuit. It was confused and lacked proper leadership, for the apes had been thrown off balance not only by the leopard's attack, but by Brandon's last gesture of defiance. But if the gorillas were no match for the situation, the leopard was still very much on the alert. Man was one of its bitterest enemies, and the sight of a human fleeing from it was too much for the spotted hell-cat to countenance. With a ten-yard spring, it left the carcase of the ape it had slaughtered, hurling itself in the wake of Brandon. Brandon caught a fleeting glimpse of its lithe shape as he glanced back for an instant. His heart came into his mouth and his throat went dry, for he knew he was in no fit condition to take on a savage leopard at this stage. Already his knees were turning to water as he plunged forward, every muscle in his tough frame crying out for rest.

If he could reach the fringe of the jungle he might stand a better chance. Putting all he knew into the effort, he staggered on, every step he took a physical battle in itself. He could hear the thud of the leopard's pads as it raced up behind him. He would never make it, he told himself. Almost, but not quite, he turned to fight his last battle.

The snarl of the leopard was loud in his ear as it moved for the final spring that would carry it straight on to Rex's back and crush him down.

Then the flat, harsh report of a high-velocity rifle splintered the air from a few yards away to Brandon's left.

He staggered and fell sprawling at the same moment, not knowing whether the shot had been meant for himself or the leopard. With his eyes closed, too exhausted to move another inch, he waited. Either the leopard would get him or another bullet would do it. He closed his eyes tightly, hearing what he thought was a snarl close behind him.

'Rex!' yelled a voice. 'Rex, laddie, are ye all right? Speak, mon, for the love o' heaven!'

Brandon opened his eyes. The jungle pressed in on one hand; the emptiness of the clearing on the other. And above him was the anxious face of McNulty, sandy hair sticking out wildly from under his hat. Brandon shifted his gaze from the Scotsman to the body of the dead leopard, less than a yard away. He got to his feet with care as McNulty reached out a hand.

'Thank you, Mac,' said Brandon thoughtfully. 'That's not the first time you've saved my life, but I think I'm a lot more grateful this time than I've ever been before.'

'Och, dinna fash y'sel'!' grunted his rescuer. 'Ye're nothing but a blamed nuisance!'

'Where's Graham?' inquired Brandon with a grin. He looked round, but there was no sign of their companion. The clearing looked as if it was full of dead gorillas, but of Graham it was empty.

'Oh, I left him across the water,' said McNulty easily. 'I reckoned I could do the job of finding you on me own!'

'Lucky you made such good time,' said Brandon grimly. 'Another five seconds and you'd have been too late!'

McNulty tilted his head to one side. 'Aye, mon,' he said; 'but I nearly didn't get here at all. There was trouble . . . terrible trouble!'

Brandon remembered the sound of shooting and shouting from across the river as he plunged after the bearded man. 'What happened?' he demanded urgently. 'I heard some fuss going on, but I reckoned you could handle almost anything yourself so kept on with what I was doing.'

McNulty started to walk about the

little clearing. He examined the bodies of the gorillas, marvelling silently when he saw that several of them had been slain with a knife. Then he turned back and eyed Brandon solemnly, the humour gone from his eyes.

'We're not so well off as we were, lad,' he said gravely. 'The men went after the drifting raft. A lot of 'em did. They were attacked by some more of these dratted apes. Most all of 'em fled, an' heaven knows when we'll see 'em again! Graham an' meself got entangled with a lion and had to kill it, but it just happened to smash our radio before we beat it. Jumped right on the thing, it did. I dinna ken what we shall do now!'

Brandon frowned. With most of the men gone and the radio smashed they were in a poor way. It would mean relying entirely on their own resources. 'Maybe Graham can mend the set later on,' he said. But he spoke very doubtfully.

McNulty shook his head. 'The spares were lost with the raft,' he said. 'No, Rex, we're out of touch and we shall stay that way. I canna see anythin' else for it.'

Brandon stifled a yawn. He was weary in mind and body, but forced himself to stand erect as he faced McNulty. 'Come on,' he said grimly. 'Let's get back and sort out the mess — unless Graham's done it already.'

'Aye, he's a good lad, is Graham,' said the Scot dourly. 'For all his fool talk he's a good lad.'

They started off, walking as fast as they could through the tangle of mangrove jungle. The journey was accomplished without mishap. Before leaving the clearing where he had fought the gorillas, Brandon collected his knife and revolver, reloading the latter in readiness for any further trouble.

Arriving at the river, they were hailed by Graham from the far bank. Brandon had been dreading the crossing, for he did not feel up to fighting off crocodiles unless he had no other alternative. The sight of Graham, however, cheered him enormously, for the man had not been wasting his time. A crude, hurriedly constructed raft lay floating on the river, and Graham was standing ready with a pole to push off across the broad expanse of water. Standing with Graham on the far bank was Muuma, McNulty's headman. Brandon also caught a glimpse of Impo, who had previously been ferried across the river by Graham during McNulty's absence.

The pleasure of the reunion was somewhat marred by the fact that the remainder of the bearers had taken to their heels and might never be seen again. Nor did Impo's wounds tend to make it an occasion for joy. However, when he examined him again, Brandon decided that a few days' rest would put him right. The injuries inflicted by the crocodile's tail were less serious than he had at first imagined.

Brandon sank to the ground with his back against a tree and relaxed. McNulty gave him his flask, telling him to 'tak' a wee drop, lad.' Brandon grinned and complied with the order.

Shortly afterwards they gathered round the pile of stores that had first been brought across before disaster struck. It was obvious that they could not hang about where they were, waiting for the men to return. The odds were that they would never return, but make for their own villages as quickly as they could. Muuma, McNulty's headman, voiced this opinion firmly. The only thing to do under the circumstances was to select essential stores and dump the rest, carrying what they needed themselves. The division was made with care, McNulty supervising.

Impo insisted that he was perfectly fit enough to travel, and Brandon was compelled to agree that the man was tough. They gathered on the river bank, staring across at the dark wall of the mangrove swamp. It seemed to curtain the country beyond with a brooding silence of its own. What it concealed none of them could say, but Brandon knew from his recent experiences that it was a country of unsuspected danger.

'Well, men, are we ready?' Graham said. He shrugged his revolver belt more securely around his waist, slapping the holster confidently.

'Aye, let's not waste more time,' said McNulty quietly.

Graham went forward and grasped the

liana rope he had tied to the hastily made raft, drawing the vessel close to the bank. McNulty started picking up the packages of gear and stores they had decided to take along with them. Muuma was helping McNulty.

Brandon went on staring across the river at the dark wall of the mangroves. Their route would lie through the heart of that wet, dank jungle. Only by following the trail of the bare-footed man could they hope to solve the mystery that surrounded the secret radio.

He glanced at Graham and the Scot. They were both fully occupied, as was Muuma. Brandon felt like saying something about the jungle across the river, but decided not to. They all had quite enough worries on their shoulders as it was, without adding to them. Brandon relapsed into thought, his eyes brooding on the far side of the turgid flow of water.

Then quite suddenly he was no longer brooding. The whole of his muscular frame stiffened instantly as he caught sight of movement at the fringe of the mangroves.

Graham was standing on the raft, stacking the equipment. McNulty was staggering down the bank with his arms full. Neither man had his rifle handy at the time. Brandon's keen eyes flicked back to the opposite bank of the river. What he saw brought him leaping to his feet, hand darting out towards Graham's rifle where it rested against a tree close by.

The figure of a woman came into view at the edge of the mangroves. She was staggering in her tracks, looking over her shoulder fearfully as she made for the river. Her clothes were in rags, and long blonde hair fell across her face. Mud and dirt streaked her skin, and she looked exhausted. It was, without doubt, the missing film star Glory Fanshawe.

Brandon raised his voice in a shout, calling to McNulty and Graham as well as the woman. 'Don't try to swim!' he yelled urgently. 'Crocs!'

Glory stopped abruptly, peering across the water in a bewildered fashion. Brandon started running towards the raft. Graham stared speechlessly at him, not realising that his attention had been directed at Glory. McNulty, however, caught on quickly. He, too, shouted to her.

Brandon reached the raft and pointed. Graham gave a gasp of dismay. 'My God!' he breathed. 'Look behind her, man!'

Brandon said nothing. Without wasting a second, he dropped to one knee and brought his rifle up to the shoulder. Creeping up at the back of the frightened, bewildered woman across the river was the enormous shape of one of Red Beard's gorillas.

The echoing report of the shot sounded flat and harsh as it leapt across the water. Glory gave a cry, perhaps thinking it was meant for her. Graham yelled to her. McNulty came running up, his rifle levelled for a second shot if Brandon had missed. But Brandon rarely missed a shot when he put his mind to it. The lumbering bulk of the ape buckled slowly at the knees as Glory turned her head in fear. With one long groaning cry, the great brute died where it fell.

Brandon lowered the rifle swiftly. 'Come on!' he said urgently. 'We've got to pick her up.'

McNulty leapt on to the raft. Brandon and Graham began to push off from the bank, leaving Muuma and Impo behind. Then the woman across the river gave a cry. The three men saw a ragged figure running from the mangroves. It was a figure with reddish hair and a beard.

Brandon cursed savagely, grabbing up his rifle again. But the bearded man stayed right behind Glory, using her as a shield. Before she could escape, he had seized her round the waist and was dragging her backwards into the opaque density of the jungle. Kicking and struggling, she disappeared from view while the three men on the raft stared after her, powerless to act.

Then Graham and Brandon were poling the raft with feverish energy. 'After them!' roared McNulty. 'We'll get that devil before we're through!'

The others did not speak, but bent to their task with a will.

9

The Secret of the Swamp

By the time they had reached the opposite bank, there was no sight or sound of the bearded man and his prisoner. Brandon sent Graham and McNulty on ahead to pick up the trail while he himself returned across the river to collect Impo and Muuma. The two men had imagined themselves to be left out of the chase, and were delighted when Brandon returned. With them they brought the rest of the stores, for Graham had not had time to load the raft properly when they first set out to rescue the film star.

It took but little time to ferry the men and the gear across stream, and then the three of them hurried in an effort to catch up with McNulty and Graham. Just as Brandon had expected, the trail, which was easy to follow, bored into the very heart of the mangrove swamp. From the sign as he and Muuma read it, it was plain that the bearded man was pushing the pace considerably. Brandon felt sorry for Glory, but was sure that eventually they would manage to wrest her from his grasp.

Impo, despite his wounded back, was putting up a fine show, so that none of them was worried about him now. But the pace was exhausting in the extreme. Even Brandon found it trying. But he knew that he must overtake Graham and the Scotsman as soon as he could.

Pushing on through the dense growth for what seemed hours, they came at last to a definite thinning of the jungle. 'The mangroves will finish soon, *bwana*,' murmured Impo stolidly.

'Good,' said Brandon. 'We might be able to see something in that case.' He wiped the sweat from his eyes and grasped Graham's rifle with renewed determination. The end of the chase might be closer than he imagined, he told himself. Both lines of footprints were still leading him on. Those of the woman showed that she was now walking at the side of her captor, so that it looked as if he had forced his will on her to a sufficient extent to make her pliable.

Presently the mangroves disappeared and gave place to tall savanna grass and acacia scrub. It was a strange little pocket of growth in the midst of jungle country, but Brandon was glad of the transformation, for now the trailing of both his enemy and his friends was a simpler matter. In fact, there were places over which he and his two native companions literally ran, for the passage of the party ahead had beaten the grass down and formed a clearly defined path.

But once again the country changed, turning back to thick tropical jungle. Brandon peered about him curiously, for he had a hunch that he had been here before. It was Impo who recognised it plainly, however.

'The hut in the *mopani* tree, sir,' he murmured wearily. 'This place is near where we found it.'

Brandon snapped his fingers. 'Of course!' he said. 'I didn't recognise it for a moment. We're in pigmy land now, so watch your step, both of you.'

'Yes, *bwana*,' Impo murmured uncertainly. Brandon hurried forward, leading his men along quickly. Sure enough, the three of them soon came in sight of the tall *mopani* tree. The leaf-and-bough hut was still there in its lower branches, but the trail passed it by. There was no sign of life to be seen in any direction, though Brandon kept his eyes skinned for traces of the savage gorillas that did Red Beard's bidding so obediently.

Plunging into the jungle again on the far side of the forest clearing, they took up the trail once more. Then Muuma stopped and sniffed the air suspiciously.

'What is it, Muuma?' queried Brandon. He had come to respect the native's uncanny instinct for trouble.

'I smell water and swamp, sir,' replied the man. 'Big swamp, I think. It will be dangerous.'

Brandon's mouth hardened. He thought he was finished with swamps for a time. 'Come on,' he muttered. 'We're sticking to this trail no matter what it leads us through!'

The natives exchanged a glance, then grinned and hurried on in the wake of Brandon. He knew he could rely on their loyalty to his cause, and the thought gave him added confidence if he needed it. Of all the bearers with the double safari, Impo and Muuma had been the only ones who had not fled back there on the other side of the river.

Slashing and hacking a way for themselves with machetes, the three men finally broke through a particularly dense belt of jungle growth and halted on the edge of a broad open space. The far side of it was curtained off by trailing lianas, and even as Brandon stopped he saw that the lianas were swinging. Catching a glimpse of what might have been a white bush shirt, he sent a shout echoing across the scrubby ground. The lianas were disturbed once more and the face of Graham broke cover. Seeing Brandon, he raised his hand in grave salute and turned to call McNulty. The little Scot appeared and the two men hurried out into the open to meet Brandon with the natives as they started across the clearing.

'Och, but it's good to see ye again, laddie!' burst out McNulty as they shook hands. Graham stood there grinning, then he glanced over his shoulder at the jungle.

'We're catching up with your bearded friend pretty fast,' he pointed out. 'Don't want to hang around, Rex. Wizard show if we catch the blighter, what?' He fingered his long curling moustache affectionately. Graham was back to normal. Brandon slapped his shoulder and laughed.

'Hot on the track of the film world, eh?' he said. 'I agree that we carry on, though.'

McNulty needed no further prompting. The whole party hastened across the clearing and plunged once more into the dim twilit world of jungle that surrounded them.

But their progress was not to be as simple as they hoped. After several hundred yards of hard going through some of the thickest stuff they had ever struck, the double trail of the bearded man and the unfortunate woman veered away from the line it had originally taken. Muuma once more sniffed the air and muttered something about a swamp. The others heard him, but took no notice beyond nodding agreement. The country was taking on a definitely steamier and hotter cloak. The air was heavy with the stagnant smells of rotting foliage and dead, damp vegetation. Heat and stickiness pressed in around them, while what small amount of light filtered down through the branches of the trees grew dimmer still.

'The tracks are very fresh now,' said Muuma, who was walking a little ahead with McNulty. 'The *mulungu* and the woman are close.'

McNulty gripped his rifle tightly and peered ahead, trying to see further into the density of growth that blocked their view.

'Swamp,' said Muuma a moment later. 'Very dangerous.'

McNulty stopped, frowning and staring round in some anxiety. 'Trail's getting difficult to follow,' he observed. 'I dinna ken which way he went.'

'Ground's getting wet,' said Brandon grimly. 'It was like this in the mangrove swamp. I lost it myself back there. Can't you find it, Muuma?'

Muuna knelt and stared at the soggy ground. His face was disappointed when he looked up. 'No, *bwana*,' he said. 'They could have gone any way. Through swamp, perhaps. Must be a path.'

McNulty swore luridly and stamped onwards, following the line the tracks had been taking when they were lost. Muuma and Impo walked along with him, while Brandon and Graham brought up the rear. The going grew worse and worse, with their feet sinking almost ankle-deep in watery mud and stinking slime. With every step they expected to find themselves treading in a bottomless morass.

'We don't even know if they came this way,' said Brandon dejectedly. 'It seems madness to carry on like this.'

'Dinna git worried, mon,' advised McNulty gravely. 'I'd like to know what else we can do. If we had an aeroplane, we might fly and see them from above!'

Graham grinned, but added nothing more to the pointless conversation. Then the mud changed abruptly to a stretch of water and slime. McNulty drew his foot back in the nick of time, just saving himself from plunging in to his neck. 'Now what?' he demanded. 'We swim, I suppose?'

'See if the men can discover anything first,' suggested Brandon. 'Impo, the bearded man and his prisoner must have come in this direction. They could not have gone anywhere else — unless they turned and doubled back on their own tracks, which would be a fool's trick. See if you can find out how they entered the swamp. A solid path, or something of that kind perhaps. And you, Muuma, try as well. We must not lose them, you understand?'

'Yes, *bwana*,' replied the two natives, speaking simultaneously.

They set off in opposite directions, skirting the very edge of the reeking swamp. Brandon and the others waited. They stared out across the noisome surface of the place. Gaunt trees of unknown variety thrust up through the green slime that coated the water. Floating logs and rotting branches protruded here and there, lifting stark fingers of black dead wood to the green roof of foliage overhead.

Brandon stiffened, seeing movement in the sullen-looking water. He touched Graham's arm and pointed. A long, serpent-like shape reared up and splashed back, half-seen but horrible for all that.

'Water snake!' he whispered. 'This is one of the most unhealthy places I've ever struck, and that's saying something. I'd hate to fall in. A man wouldn't stand a chance.'

Graham shuddered violently. 'Nasty spot for a prang,' he said.

Brandon was about to say something when a shout from Impo took his whole attention. McNulty gave a grunt of satisfaction, starting off at a fast pace with the others in his wake.

They found Impo bending down on the edge of the swamp, studying some faintly discernible marks in the soft mud. 'The *mulungu* used a boat, *bwana*,' he said, glancing up to meet their eager gaze. 'Canoe. He pushed off from here and went across the water. Snakes in there. Bad place. This is bad juju country.'

Brandon ignored the last part of the

142

information. He already knew it was bad country without being told again. 'So he had a canoe waiting, did he?' he mused. 'Well, that puts us in something of a spot, doesn't it?' He looked round at his companions. They frowned and stared at the unfriendly surface of the still swamp before them.

'Isn't there something we can do?' Graham voiced the thoughts of all of them. It seemed disastrous to be baulked at this stage when they were so close to the end of the chase. To admit defeat in the face of a stretch of water and mud was unthinkable, yet none of them could see a way out of their difficulties.

Brandon tipped his sun helmet to the back of his head and scratched his head, frowning as he did so. He did not like to think of the bearded man somewhere across the swamp, nor did he relish the idea of the film star in his hands. 'We've got to do something quickly!' he said with sudden determination. 'Maybe this isn't as deep as it looks. There is just a chance that if we feel our way carefully, we can cross without a boat.'

'Och, lad, ye're mad to talk such nonsense,' said McNulty harshly.

'I could make a raft,' said Muuma. His eyes showed the fear he felt at the prospect of actually wading into the swamp. He would have been willing to make a raft out of anything to avoid such a procedure.

McNulty glanced at him keenly. 'Can ye do it, mon?'

'Yes, sir, as I say,' replied Muuma with a violent nod of his head.

'Then get cracking,' said Graham with a sigh of relief. 'I must say I hate the idea of walking into that stuff. I don't suppose for a moment we'd come out alive if we did.'

Brandon said nothing, but the necessary delay irked him, though he knew they would stand a better chance of success if they could build a raft for the trip.

They all set to with a will, hacking down stems of jungle growth and lashing them together with strands of liana. When it was finished — which was done considerably quicker than any of them had expected — the raft was a flimsy enough affair, but by careful management promised to support their combined weight for the crossing.

Propelled by two poles, the vessel started off. It creaked and weaved as the natives thrust it forward through the water. Brandon crouched at the front end, his rifle balanced across his knees, ready for an instant shot if danger threatened them from the depths of the swamp. Behind him, Graham and McNulty stood up, McNulty with a rifle, Graham armed with his revolver.

'Where are we heading?' queried Graham.

'Straight across as far as we can get,' answered Brandon. 'We don't know where they've gone, but we're sure to make a landfall of some sort before very long. This swamp can't extend indefinitely.'

'Don't you believe it!' retorted McNulty curtly. 'This is more like the end of the world than African country!'

Brandon grinned, but did not take his eyes from the green surface ahead. Suddenly it erupted violently. The long sinuous shape of a giant water snake reared up, ploughing towards the craft.

Brandon lifted his rifle as Muuma let out a cry of warning. Taking careful aim, he squeezed the trigger, cursing as he did so at the necessity of firing, for the report would be sure to give away their position to the bearded man. However, the snake was fully thirty feet in length, and would have had no difficulty in tearing the raft into pieces if it chose to coil round it.

The crash of the shot seemed to roll across the swamp for minutes on end, echoing back and forth among the gaunt trees that grew from the slime. The giant water snake, writhing and twisting as it felt the deadly impact of the bullet, finally disappeared in a last violent flurry. It was less than a stone's throw from the raft when it died.

'Nice shooting, old man,' said Graham appreciatively. 'Positively bang on!'

McNulty grunted, realising the danger that Brandon's shot might have stirred for them all. But he knew it had had to be done and raised no objection.

Muuma and Impo continued to drive the flimsy raft forward. Graham and McNulty steered it through and round the growth of odd-looking trees that sprang up from the bed of the swamp. They managed to keep to a more or less straight course in spite of the many twists and turns they were forced to make. Then the water shallowed with unexpected rapidity. The fairly open growth through which they had been thrusting grew denser and changed abruptly to the thick green wall of jungle.

'Solid land ahead,' said Brandon quietly. 'Can you see where they're likely to have landed, Impo?' He stood up at the front of the raft and shaded his eyes with his hand.

Impo came forward beside him. The raft was close to the wall of the jungle by this time. Nothing disturbed the silence and stillness of the scene. McNulty took Impo's place with one of the poles, slowly edging the raft closer in to the shore. The air hung thick and moist all round them.

Impo stared ahead, then peered from side to side along the narrow stretch of solid ground that was visible. There were no traces of a boat having grounded on the mud. 'Never mind,' said Graham. 'We can cast round for spoor when we land, just as we found out where they started from. Nothing to it, old boy!'

Brandon hid a faint smile, but his thoughts were grim. If they failed to pick up the tracks of the bearded man and his film star captive, it would not be a cheerful prospect for anyone concerned. He said nothing, however, not wishing to damp Graham's spirits.

'Aye,' said McNulty soberly. 'We'd best get on dry land for a start, as you say, laddie. All together now . . . Heave!' They thrust at the poles, then Brandon leapt for the shelving mud bank ahead and splashed through the fringe of under-growth. The raft grounded violently, creaking as it did so. Brandon turned to see the others jumping ashore. They gathered on the bank, peering round anxiously.

'Impo, Muuma, try to pick up tracks,' ordered McNulty.

The two men nodded quickly, separat-ing and starting to follow the edge of the swamp, eyes bent to the ground. The others stayed where they were. They did not want to be separated under the circumstances, and the natives were far more qualified to track than they were, though Brandon himself was no slouch when it came to spoor-finding.

For what seemed a long time all was quiet, only the faint chatter of the birds breaking the torrid stillness. Then the three waiting men stiffened suddenly as the air rang with a loud cry of fear and alarm.

'Muuma!' grunted McNulty. 'Come on! He doesn't yell that way unless he's in bad trouble!'

They had crashed their way through the undergrowth, hard on the path Muuma had taken when he left. Brandon hesitated for an instant, then sent out a call for Impo to follow them. Running hard, his clothes almost torn from his back by the vicious thorn scrub and hanging branches of acacia, he followed the other two.

Suddenly they halted, the sound of their movement gone. Brandon was close behind them now. He broke through a screen of foliage and came to an abrupt halt. But it was too late to back away.

McNulty and Graham were surrounded by a horde of pigmies, threatened by spears from every angle and covered by bows and arrows. Muuma had been seized and overcome, and Brandon was surrounded before he could put up a fight. The entire party were captives, all but Impo.

10

Captive!

The scene was one to strike terror into the hearts of most men, but Brandon forced himself to remain his usual calm self. How many of the pigmy warriors there were he did not know, but it was obvious at a glance that he and his men could not hope to put up a fight and get away with their lives.

What appeared to have happened was that Muuma, following the edge of the swamp, had been surprised. It seemed to Brandon that the pigmies had been waiting for just such an occurrence, and the fact that Brandon had shot the water snake had in all probability concentrated the natives in this area. If the bearded man was in the vicinity — as Brandon thought he must be — he was likely to have despatched his hordes to intercept pursuit. Brandon stiffened as a dozen of the warriors pressed in round him, their short, sharp spears actually pricking his skin.

He could have shot down several of them, but a swift glance from McNulty decided him not to risk it, for such a move would only have ended in the loss of his own life. The others, too, would probably have suffered the same fate. Since they already had Muuma and his two companions tightly grasped, there was nothing to do but surrender.

With a silent oath, Brandon allowed himself to be seized by the arms. His rifle was taken, but none of the pigmies seemed to realise that he carried a revolver. That fact, he thought, might come in useful later on.

McNulty said: 'Don't lose heart, laddies! They've got us, but they may not keep us for long.'

Graham scowled at the men who grasped him firmly. 'It's my idea that they'll take us to their boss,' he put in. 'What do you say, Rex?'

Brandon grinned despite the serious-ness of the position. 'What I say is unprintable. But you're right about our destination. They haven't killed us, so the odds are they've got orders not to.'

Muuma sent a look of appeal to his employer, but McNulty only shook his head warningly.

Without more ado, the captives were hustled along a narrow path through the jungle. Creeping plants and dense thorn almost completely barred the way, but the pigmies beat a path with their spears, hacking and slicing at the foliage as they went. There must have been forty or fifty of them, Brandon decided. He was troubled by the realisation that these people, normally so peaceable and friendly, should have turned violent at the bidding of one foreign man. The threat of The Fury was no empty promise, it seemed. Brandon's blood ran cold when he pictured the havoc Red Beard could wreak in the vast lands of Africa. The threat would eventually be brought under control, of course, but it could destroy a lot of men before being crushed; and he knew well enough that there were powers in the world who would go to any lengths to achieve the lessening of strength among their rivals.

To break out from their present predicament was out of the question, for the pigmy warriors gave them no rope at all. Although still partly armed, Brandon and his men were as helpless to overcome this mass of hostile warriors as if they had lost all their weapons. And the pigmies seemed to know it.

Brandon glanced around at the men in his immediate vicinity, hoping perhaps to see some he recognised; but there was not a face he knew by sight. He began to think these men must be from some different tribe from the ones who had captured himself and Impo previously. The thought of Impo gave him a faint hope of assistance, for he knew that his man would do all he could to release them if the opportunity came. But Impo would first of all have to trail them, and Impo was wounded. What could he do against such numbers?

Brandon said nothing of all this to his comrades in danger. He kept his thoughts to himself and refused to bank on them too much, but they were still at the back of his mind when the long procession finally broke out from the dense jungle country and straggled across a big clearing of flat, dry earth.

The four prisoners looked about them, wondering if it was worth the risk of making a break for it. But the pack of warriors around them was half a dozen deep, and the blades of a score of spears were pointing straight at them. To attempt a run for freedom would be suicidal at this stage.

Out in front were another handful of pigmies, while the rear of the triumphant party was brought up by more. The only sound that broke the silence of the jungle clearing was the soft thud of a hundred feet, bare on the ground.

On the far side of the clearing they plunged into jungle again, but this time they were using a well-defined path, hard underfoot and broad enough for three or four men to walk abreast. It was obviously far more than a game trail, and must have been cut fairly recently.

Brandon said: 'It looks as if we're getting near to operations H.Q., Graham.'

Graham nodded. 'I'd give a lot for just one little tommy-gun,' he answered. 'Or a hand grenade.'

'Might as well wish for the stars,' put in McNulty sourly. 'If we had an atom bomb, they'd kill us before we could use it. Mon, but I'm gettin' thirsty!'

Brandon unslung his water canteen from his shoulder and passed it over to the Scotsman. The pigmies made no effort to prevent his move.

McNulty snorted. 'Och, mon, I said a drink!' he said, waving the canteen aside disgustedly. 'Not water!'

Brandon shrugged. Graham grinned and pulled out his flask, passing it to McNulty in silence. The geologist accepted it with a grateful sigh.

Brandon, for want of anything better to do, stared at their captors curiously. As they progressed further and further along the broad jungle path, it became evident that the pigmies were growing uneasy and nervous.

'They may be obedient to Red Beard,' said Brandon, 'but he scares the daylights out of them.'

'Aye, I've been noticin' that,' answered McNulty grimly.

'What we ought to have is a barrel of salt,' said Graham. 'I've heard tell these little gentlemen are willing to kill their grandmothers for a handful of salt.'

Brandon grunted. 'We haven't any salt,' he said flatly.

'Oh, I know that; it was just an idea.'

'Keep it for later.'

The jungle path ended in a circular space among the *baobob* trees, acacia scrub and tall *mopanis*. A rich display of tropical flowers were banked round the edge of the clearing, while situated on the far side, occupying a slight rise in the ground, was a large and imposing thatched hut. It was really more than a hut, for its floor space must have been equal to many of the bungalows found in towns. Standing in the doorway, beneath the shade of the roof, with his arms folded across his chest and legs planted wide, was the red-bearded man.

Visibly frightened, the pigmy warriors at last brought their prisoners to a halt at the bottom of the wooden steps that gave access to the veranda of the hut. Many of them bowed their heads almost to the ground.

The bearded man picked up a rifle and covered his prisoners, grinning down at them all the time. None of them spoke, each waiting for their enemy to make the first move. But before addressing his captives, the bearded man gave a sharp command to the pigmies who surrounded them. He told them to leave him, but first to take all the guns they could find on the captives.

Brandon and his companions were quickly relieved of their revolvers and other weapons. Then the bearded man picked on two of the pigmies, telling them to bring the prisoners inside the hut. The remainder he dismissed. Brandon, seeing the way in which they scuttled off, was reminded again that this was a rule of fear, not affection.

Disarmed, the captives were herded up the steps of the veranda and prodded through the doorway under the watchful eye of the bearded man. There was a triumphant sneer on his lips all the time, but he did not deign to speak for a long time when he had them where he wanted them — standing with their backs against the wall of the room with the light in their eyes so that he could study them at leisure.

'So,' he said at last. 'You have the effrontery to meddle in my affairs, yes?' His foreign accent was very noticeable now, more so than it had been when Brandon heard him speaking last.

McNulty stuck his chin out defiantly. 'Aye,' he snapped curtly. 'But I wouldn't call it meddlin', mister! You're heading straight for the gallows, and we only want to help you on your way!'

The man only smiled, swaying slightly where he stood, the barrel of his rifle sweeping the line of their faces. 'This is an automatic weapon,' he murmured gently. 'I only have to squeeze the trigger and I shoot you down one at a time. For every squeeze a dead man! It is easy, is it not?'

'Easy to talk!' retorted Graham. 'What the hell do you think you're trying to do, anyway? If you killed us now, it wouldn't do you any good. The secret of your radio is known. We're only a small advance party, Red Beard! We really came after you when we found out you'd captured Glory Fanshawe.'

'The other man I killed was only an advance party,' said their captor grimly. 'He would not talk and I did not even know his name, but he meddled in my business. Now he is dead. He escaped from me, but he was dying when he got away. It is well, yes?'

'You swine!' grated Brandon, clenching his fists. Had he had a revolver at his waist he would have risked all in a wild attempt to slay this taunting man.

'I've been called that before,' was the answer. 'Words do not wound, my brave cockatoo! They cannot harm as a bullet can, yes?' He smiled, and the smile was as ugly as any that the prisoners had ever seen.

'Who are ye, an' where do ye come from?' demanded McNulty.

'I am the one who will ask the questions.'

They glared back at him in silence,

caught without an answer in the face of his attitude. Then Brandon touched his tongue to his lips and shifted his feet on the floor. The floor was of beaten earth, raised and packed above the normal ground level outside. As with many other tiny details of his surroundings, Brandon took the fact without thinking about it and stored it away for future reference. 'You're a fool, of course,' he said slowly. 'If you wipe us out it won't gain you anything. We've already sent a radio message of our approximate location.'

'Bluff, Britisher! Fool's bluff, and I call it! The radio set you boast about was lost when my army of gorillas attacked your camp some time ago. I know nearly everything that happens in the Congo jungle, and you cannot try to fool me.'

'You're fooling yourself,' snapped Graham shortly.

'Who are you?' Brandon asked their captor.

'A man of importance in my own country,' came the answer. 'I am here in the jungle for a purpose, but I am not cut off from my government. Word travels easily enough, so that I know every move before it is made; can prepare for the moment most suitable for striking at the rotten foundations of your rule in Africa!'

His eyes were blazing with an unholy light. Brandon saw with some uneasiness that his trigger finger was white where it squeezed in his excitement. The rifle swung from side to side in an arc that covered them all in turn. How much longer would it go on? he wondered.

'Mon, ye're scatty!' exploded McNulty. He took a step away from the wall, but the fanatic's rifle brought him up short, quivering in the grip of the man who held it.

'Don't force me to kill you till I am ready!' came the curt command. 'There may be possible uses for men of your type when the moment of rising comes.' He glared round. 'You are all fools; but you have a sort of courage. Perhaps we can make a deal presently — when I am ready. It will benefit yourselves and save me considerable trouble.'

'Save your breath,' advised Graham coldly. 'We may be fools as you say, but we're none of us traitors!'

The bearded man whirled round, teeth bared in a snarl. 'Silence!' he roared. 'Silence, or I kill you where you stand!'

Graham yawned loudly, then smoothed his moustache. 'Have it your own way,' he drawled.

'Where is the woman?' asked Brandon, changing the subject abruptly. He admired Graham's nerve, but did not want to hasten death by insults.

The bearded man took a grip on himself. He sneered. 'Where she is safe and can do no harm,' he replied. 'I shall have a special place for her when the great rising comes. I shall break her spirit and make her my queen! Together we shall represent my mighty government on this continent!'

'Glad to hear it,' drawled Graham. 'Bang on, what?'

'Enough of this!' snarled their captor. He was clearly developing an intense dislike for Graham. Before any of them could speak again, the man bawled an order over his shoulder. Four of the pigmies appeared as if by magic, bowing low to the floor in front of their over-bearing master. He spoke to them harshly, giving orders in their own tongue, Brandon listened intently, for he knew the language well.

The prisoners were driven into another room of the hut at the point of spears, with the bearded man bringing up the rear with the ever-ready rifle. The second room they entered was completely bare of any furnishings. Brandon caught sight of a square wooden trap in the floor. They were halted close to it while the man gave further orders. Two of the pigmies struggled to raise the trap door. It required their combined strength. Then they stood aside and waited, taking up their spears once more and menacing the captives with them.

'Down there you will sleep in peace!' said the man with a dry laugh. 'It is a long drop, so be careful. There are no facilities in this place for mending broken bones.'

'Where's my parachute?' grumbled Graham.

'Get down before I shoot you down!' roared the man in a sudden fury.

'Better go,' murmured Brandon. He stepped close to the edge of the black hole that yawned in front of them. He could see nothing whatever below. The drop might have been a mile for all the indication he had.

Kneeling on the edge, he turned and swung his legs over. They encountered air. Holding his breath, he let go with his hand, falling. When he stopped falling he did so heavily, rolling over on a hard floor with a jar that almost winded him. A moment later Graham landed beside him. Then McNulty and Muuma.

The trap door slammed shut above their heads.

11

The Cellar

No one spoke for several seconds, then McNulty started moving about cautiously.

'Now this 'ere is the hunderground dungeon where Sir Walter Raleigh was himprisoned for many long years, ladies and gents,' Graham spoke in sepulchral tones.

Brandon grinned in the darkness. 'For Pete's sake, spare us the details!' he said.

'Sorry, old lad,' said Graham. 'What do we do now?'

'Find out something about our prison,' answered Brandon. He began to creep in a straight line till his outstretched fingers encountered the warm earth of the wall. By moving along it a little way, he ran into McNulty.

'Look where ye're goin', mon,' said the Scot.

'Stand just there and don't move,' countered Brandon. He passed McNulty

166

and made a complete circuit of the walls till he reached the Scotsman again.

'Well?' queried Graham from the gloom. 'How big?'

'Near enough twenty feet square,' replied Brandon. 'But I can't reach the roof anywhere.'

'Anybody got a light?' asked Graham. 'I've lost my matches somewhere.'

Brandon felt in his pocket. 'Never thought of that,' he said ruefully. He nicked a pocket lighter into life, but the tiny flame did little to relieve the intense darkness. However, it was better than no light at all, and they were able to make out the beamed roof of the cellar some ten feet above the floor.

'It's certain that we can't get out through the trap,' said McNulty. 'There was a great heavy bolt across it when they lifted it.'

'What else can we do?' asked Graham. 'If we had a spade we could dig our way out.'

'We haven't got a spade,' said Brandon patiently.

'Aye, laddie, but we've all got our

hands!' put in McNulty. 'We could dig with them. This is only dirt, after all.'

Brandon had been thinking along similar lines. The only trouble was that he did not know which wall to start on. If they dug a tunnel it would have to be a short one, coming out above ground at the rear of the big hut. Anything else would be useless. But what with falling down into the cellar, and walking about it afterwards, he had lost all sense of direction in relation to the upper world.

Graham, however, insisted that the wall nearest the spot where they were standing was the one to excavate. Since they could not argue against the choice, they were forced to accept it. A few seconds later the work had been started.

McNulty was the only one among them who had anything in the nature of a tool, and in view of the fact that this was nothing but a very small penknife the task seemed hopeless. Progress was painfully slow, and at the end of ten minutes' labour they had only scratched a small depression in the hard-packed earth that formed the wall. 'We'll take a month at this rate,' grumbled Graham in a tone of dismay.

'Red Beard won't give us a month,' answered Brandon curtly. 'We've got to make the best of it.'

Taking turns with the penknife, they scratched and dug on for what seemed ages. The tunnel, if it could yet be called by such a name, slanted upwards from the cellar floor. It was now about two feet in length, but the men were tiring. Their hands and fingers were raw, and the little knife was beginning to give out under the strain. Presently McNulty, at the working face, grunted disgustedly.

'What's up?' demanded Graham.

'The blade's come out, laddie. That's what's up!'

They gathered round, Brandon lighting the lighter again. What McNulty had said was true. The small blade of the knife had broken loose from the swivel rivet that held it. They mended it with difficulty and carried on, but it soon became clear that the knife was more or less useless. They spent more time mending it than using it now.

Brandon sat back on his heels and frowned. His hands were bleeding and sweat had soaked his clothes. Muuma, who had done his share of the work with the rest, sank back exhausted beside him. McNulty and Graham leaned against the wall. No one spoke, their thoughts too bitter for words. Even Brandon could not trust his voice.

Suddenly Muuma shifted his body and grew tense. In the utter darkness Brandon sensed the man's bated breath.

'What?' he whispered.

Muuma's hand touched his wrist for silence. 'Listen, *bwana*,' he breathed. 'I hear a strange noise.'

Brandon strained his ears. Sure enough, he picked up what sounded like a distant thudding. It was faint and irregular, with gaps in it that made no sense.

'What the devil is it?' muttered Graham.

'Don't know, but it seems to be getting louder. Either that or I'm hearing things.' Brandon leaned back against the wall, listening intently. The rest of them were rigid. Dust from the wall flaked off and trickled down Brandon's neck. He brushed it off irritably. Then more fell. Suddenly a small pebble rattled down, hitting his neck and bouncing off. The faint thudding was louder.

'Mac!' whispered Brandon. 'Come here quickly!' Turning to glance at the wall, he had noticed that it shook very slightly in time with the thuds. Putting his ear close against it, he listened. Dust and tiny stones were coming off it in a constant shower now.

'What do you make of it?' asked Graham.

'We're not the only tunnellers!' answered Brandon grimly. There was a sudden note of elation in his voice as he went on: 'I'll bet you anything you like that's Impo at work! He must have followed us and guessed what had happened. He might even have been able to see where we were put!'

McNulty seized his penknife again and started digging frantically at the loosened earth of the wall. A crack was appearing in it now as Brandon held the lighter aloft. They tore at the earth with their hands, helping McNulty to widen the crack. Then without any warning a large chunk broke away and thudded at their feet. McNulty started back in alarm as something flashed out and almost struck his face. Brandon gave a delighted exclamation, darting forward and grabbing hold of the spade as it widened the gap.

'Impo!' he whispered urgently. 'Is that you?'

The spade disappeared and there was dead silence beyond. They waited with bated breath, not daring to speak. Stones and earth rattled in the small hole. Then the spade was used to make it bigger still. Brandon raised the flame of his lighter and held it close to the hole, peering in anxiously. His eyes encountered those of a white-faced, grimy-looking woman.

'Hello,' she said weakly. 'I'd almost given up.' For a moment Brandon did not know whether to be pleased or disappointed. After thinking that Impo had found a way of releasing them, it was a bitter blow to discover that their visitor was none other than Glory Fanshawe, a prisoner like themselves. Then he realised that her coming was of vital importance.

She had a spade, and that would make all the difference to their efforts.

'Glad to see you,' he said. 'Pass the spade through. I'll soon make the hole big enough for you.'

She did as he asked, while Graham and McNulty stood by and watched. With a few slicing cuts Brandon quickly enlarged the tunnel she had made, then they were helping her through and into their own cellar.

The woman sank to the floor with a weary sigh. McNulty took the spade from Brandon and started work on the tunnel again. Graham knelt beside the woman and offered his flask. She took a gulp from it gratefully.

'I take it you dug a way through from another cellar,' said Brandon. 'You were lucky, but we'll all get out now we have a spade.'

She pulled a wry face. 'I thought I was digging out to freedom,' she whispered. 'Now I'm glad I took the wrong direction. The wall between the cellars was nearly ten feet thick. I didn't know you'd be here of course.' She shuddered. 'Oh, it's been awful these last weeks!'

'What happened?' asked Brandon gently.

'Well, it all began when I went out shooting with a friend I was working with,' she said. 'Something rushed at us from the bush and I panicked, running away. Pat came after me, of course, but I never saw him again. I ran through a lot of jungle stuff and stumbled on a red-headed man. It was quite unexpected, but when I saw what he was doing I got frightened. That was after I asked him for help.'

'What was he doing?'

'Unpacking a lot of machine guns from one of those parachute container things. I saw it all, naturally, and then he wouldn't let me go. He brought me here and slung me into this cellar. Every now and then he would bring me up and talk about making me a queen. He's a bit mad, I think. I tried to escape several times, but those awful apes he keeps, and the pigmies, stopped me. Then I did make a break early this morning. That was when I saw you across the river. But he caught me again. When he got me back, he was so busy that he told two of his pigmies to put me back in the cellar. By sheer luck they opened up the wrong one, I suppose, because I found a spade in the other one. The rest you know.'

'So the arms dump is not a fairy story,' mused Graham. 'Miss Fanshawe, you've confirmed some vital facts. We're much obliged to you, but our job is to get out of here as soon as we can. If we make it, could you take us to the place where you saw him unpacking guns?'

She shook her head. 'I couldn't. It might be anywhere as far as I'm concerned. I was hopelessly lost, you see.'

'Pity. Never mind; it can't be helped.'

'He's dangerous, I'm sure,' she said. 'If he hadn't decided to keep me as a sort of plaything for later on, he'd have killed me before now.'

'Didn't he tell you anything else?' asked Brandon.

She nodded in the faint glow from the lighter. 'He was always boasting when he had me out of the cellar,' she said. 'He's been a circus animal tamer once upon a time, I think. I don't know anything more about him, and I will admit that he's never actually harmed me all the time I've been a captive. But it wasn't pleasant, even so.'

Brandon was about to make some other remark when, without any warning, there was a crash above their heads and light flooded down into the cellar. The face of the bearded man was framed in the trap-door opening. He held a rifle in his hands and was grinning evilly.

'So you've met the lady, have you?' he sneered. 'I am sorry, but it will be a brief acquaintance for you. I have just received orders to hold no prisoners.'

McNulty came out of the tunnel he was digging. 'What does that mean?' he demanded.

The man above laughed gutturally, throwing his head back.

'So you'd try to dig your way out, would you?' he roared. 'Rats, the lot of you. Burrowing rats!'

Before they could answer, he spoke across his shoulder. Two of the pigmies appeared, dropping a ladder down to the floor of the cellar. 'Come up!' ordered their captor.

They obeyed slowly, Brandon going first, followed by Graham, then McNulty, still clutching the spade, with Muuma and Glory bringing up the rear.

The bearded man laughed, struck at McNulty with the butt of his rifle and knocked the spade from his grasp, bringing a curse from the Scotsman's tight mouth. They were lined up against the wall of the room, then the pigmies tied their arms with thin cord that cut deep in their flesh.

'The moment of rising is near,' the man told them. 'In a short while now the natives of Africa will be armed and will smite the white men! Chaos and bloodshed will be rife all over the continent. You, with your petty attempts to crush me, will have failed. But before you die, it is well that you know what the future may hold for your fellow countrymen!'

'Ye're as crazy as a coot,' snapped McNulty.

'We shall see,' was the answer. 'And now I must bid you goodbye. It is a shame that the woman has to die, but she knows too much and is far too stubborn to bend to my will.'

None of them spoke. The pigmies were reinforced by a dozen of their fellows, and they crowded into the room and surrounded the bound captives. Thrust outside and down the steps of the hut, they were herded along the broad jungle pathway with scant ceremony.

'Where are we being taken, do you think?' asked Glory.

Brandon did not answer. He already had a suspicion, and the thought of their possible destination did not make him any easier in his mind. The air was thick with the rank smell of the swamp. They were nearing it rapidly now. Brandon glanced over his shoulder. Striding along some distance behind them came the bearded man, his rifle never far from a constant aim at their backs.

Penetrating the dense mass of vegetation that faced them, the party and their guards moved closer and closer to the stinking expanse of the swamp. Its decaying breath seemed to reach out to meet them, enveloping them with the promise of its fearful green depths, a bottomless grave from which their bodies would never be recovered even if they were traced to its very edge.

Brandon gritted his teeth to keep down despair from flooding his mind. The future was as grim as the fury that threatened to sweep the vast spaces of Africa.

12

The Reckoning

Dusk was falling rapidly by the time the party reached the edge of the swamp and halted. The pigmy warriors waited for further orders from the bearded man.

Brandon exchanged a glance with McNulty, but there was little or no hope in the Scotsman's eyes as he met his gaze. As for Glory, although she did not fully realise the dread of their plight and approaching fate, she was frightened.

The bearded man came up and sneered at them, cradling his rifle affectionately. 'You know your fate?' he whispered. 'It will be a very suitable one for meddlers such as you.'

'And what do ye reckon to do?' demanded McNulty. 'Toss us into that filth an' let us drown before your eyes?'

Glory shuddered and let out a sob of fear. Graham looked towards her in the gathering gloom. His eyes begged her to hang on to what courage she had left. With a supreme effort, she straightened up and flung her head back defiantly. A faint smile hovered on her lips as she met Graham's eyes.

The bearded man laughed at the interplay, sensing their thoughts and feelings and fear as he watched. He was in no hurry to break up the party; that was obvious. Brandon wondered how long he would prolong the agony.

'Toss you into the swamp?' echoed their captor. 'No, I do not do things so crudely. It would not be lingering enough for the punishment you deserve. I have other plans.'

'Get on with it then,' snapped McNulty irritably. 'We're tired of standing around for your benefit.'

Again the bearded man laughed, but a moment later he gave a curt order to the pigmies, who waited in nervous silence. Brandon, listening, understood. He shivered with a wave of involuntary fear, for the man's command made his plan quite obvious.

Some of the pigmies disappeared hurriedly while the rest went on waiting. Presently there was a rustling sound in the undergrowth and a noise of hacking spear blades. The pigmies returned, bearing long boughs in their arms. Others had cut down lengths of lianas and were coiling them into rope.

'You begin to understand?' snarled the bearded man.

'Perhaps.' Brandon's voice was cold. His jaws felt stiff as he spoke. The pigmies were working fast. While the prisoners watched, they fashioned a square framework of boughs, lashing them together with lianas. When it was ready they stood back and looked at their master with dark, expectant eyes. He nodded gravely, turning again to the captives.

'It will float,' he said slowly. 'And you will be tied to it. It will float and support your bodies in the swamp, giving the water snakes and leeches and other foul things a chance to feast themselves on your flesh before you die!'

'You monster!' gasped Graham. 'Why don't you kill us quickly and have done with it?'

'Because it suits me to think of you dying slowly while I sit safe in my bungalow and work out the final details for the coming revolution!' He laughed again. 'It will do me good,' he added. 'It will make up for the loss of the woman. I would keep her alive, but I have to take orders myself. To disobey is to die!' He broke off and barked another order to the pigmies.

The prisoners were seized and thrown onto the flimsy open-work raft. With their combined weight it would only just remain afloat. Brandon almost wished it would fail to do that, for the frightful picture conjured up by the bearded man's words struck terror into his heart. Only by iron control of his will did he conceal his feelings and glare back defiantly at their tormentor.

The raft-like framework was lying on the edge of the swamp. One by one the prisoners, their legs now lashed together, were fastened to it by ropes. Two bigger boughs were then secured to the raft to give it extra buoyancy under the bearded man's direction. Then he ordered the pigmies to float it away from the edge of the bank.

The warm, thick water lapped round Brandon's back and neck as the raft splashed sluggishly out under the impulse of many willing hands. Glory gave a shuddering gasp as something soft and slimy slithered across her bare legs. Graham swore quietly and bitterly. McNulty bit his lower lip and stared upwards at the bearded man as he stood on the bank, a savage grin of triumph on his face.

'*Bon voyage*,' he sneered. 'I regret this move, but it is quite essential, of course. Goodbye, meddlers!'

The doomed prisoners did not deign to reply. For the most part they were too frightened to speak — or too bitter. The flimsy structure of boughs creaked and groaned as it slowly drifted further and further from the edge of the swamp. Darkness was coming down swiftly. In a few moments the trees and dense undergrowth were lost to view, swallowed in the thickly rolling gloom and night mist that welled from the surface of the swamp.

From out of the darkness came a

ringing laugh, derisive and sneering. Once again the bearded man bade them: '*Bon voyage!*'

Only the gurgling voice of the swamp itself broke the stillness. Lukewarm water lapped round and over their bodies. Brandon felt the sudden bite of a leech as the creature fixed on his arm. He and his companions were almost completely submerged. Glory gave a sobbing cry as some creeping thing crossed her body.

'Steady,' said Brandon grimly. 'Is anyone loosely tied enough to get free?'

Silence answered his words. He could hear McNulty grunting as he strained at his bonds, but he knew instinctively that the effort would be a wasted one. The pigmies had made sure they were fast.

There was nothing to do but wait for the end. Their nerves were so much on edge with the suspense that even a brushing of water on their skins brought gasps to their lips. McNulty went on struggling in silence with his bonds. The action threatened to upset the raft altogether, so after a while he gave it up in despair.

Then there was a faint grinding noise that jarred the entire structure. Brandon held his breath, thinking it was one of the enormous water snakes which had finally located them.

'All right,' breathed Graham. 'We've got entangled with a bough in the water. If only we could get loose, I'd willingly swim to the bank.'

'So would we all.'

Their voices echoed strangely in the thick intensity of gloom that hemmed them in. What with the darkness and mist, it was impossible to see more than a yard or two; and the fact that they were lying on their backs made matters even worse.

'Listen!' whispered Brandon after a moment or two.

They strained their ears, not knowing what to expect. A faint splashing sound reached them, gradually coming closer.

'Water snake!' grunted McNulty.

'Can't be sure,' breathed Brandon. 'It doesn't sound quite right for that somehow. This is a hellish place!'

'I'm scared,' muttered Glory. 'Oh, I

wish I was dead!'

The splashing sound ceased abruptly. Suspense swept over them again. It grew so bad that Muuma uttered a wail of unearthly fear.

'Quiet!' snapped Brandon impatiently. 'You'll bring every filthy thing that crawls over to us, Muuma.' The native subsided into silence.

The splashing sound began again, creeping towards them across the still surface of the unseen water. Glory gave a stifled cry as some creature of the swamp touched her skin with a slimy flick.

'God, I can't stand this!' muttered Graham. Brandon kept his nerves under control with difficulty. He opened his mouth to speak to Graham, then snapped it shut. From the darkness close by a shape bulked out, without substance or outline. Glory saw it and whimpered in terror, biting her lower lip to keep back a scream. Brandon cursed aloud, not knowing what this monster might be. It hovered near them for a second or two, then moved in more closely.

'Make no noise,' said a whispered

voice. 'It is I, Impo. Stay quiet, for the bad *mulungu* must not know.'

'Impo!' breathed Brandon. 'Heavens, man, I've never been so glad to hear your voice in all my life! Get us out of this, for the love of Mike!'

The others were too speechless with amazement to make a murmur. Glory was sobbing brokenly now, her reserve of courage overwhelmed by the sound of another human voice.

Impo came closer, poling a raft with the utmost care. Leaning over at a precarious angle, he started slashing at their bonds with the spear he carried. They could see him clearly now. Brandon realised what outstanding courage Impo must have called on to venture into the swamp alone in search of them.

'I was watching when they brought you to the water, *bwana*,' Impo whispered. 'I could not attack, so I waited. When the bad *mulungu* was gone with his warriors, I made a raft and came to find you.'

They were all whispering now, their spirits returned and fresh determination filling them. Freed from the structure of boughs, they carefully transferred to Impo's raft, then made for the shore from which they had recently been cast off.

'Now listen,' said Brandon quietly as they landed. 'The next part of the programme is a one-man job. I'm going after Red Beard — alone.'

They protested, argued, objected, but Brandon would have nothing said against the plan. He knew the jungle well, and McNulty must remain with the others until he returned.

With an ill grace, they conceded the point. Leaving Glory in Graham's care, with McNulty and the two natives to guard them, Brandon set off swiftly through the darkness. He carried Impo's spear, a pigmy weapon the headman had picked up in the jungle. Impo, it seemed, had arrived on the scene shortly after their capture; he had followed them to the hut in the clearing, but had been unable to approach closely enough to effect a rescue. Waiting and watching, he had again followed when they were brought to the swamp.

Brandon covered the distance as

quickly as he could. The going was anything but good in the density of the night, but his instinctive sense of direction aided him considerably. By the time he saw the dark shape of the bungalow hut ahead, less than an hour had passed since leaving his companions.

Pausing and listening intently, he saw a light flicker into life through the doorway of the hut. Red Beard was at home, he thought grimly. With the utmost care he advanced, every sense on the alert. Crossing the edge of the big clearing, he slid into the fringe of forest undergrowth, passing round the clearing and edging in towards the rear of the hut. When he reached it, he stopped to listen again. A faint humming sound came to his ears, making him frown.

There was a doorway in the back of the hut. A chink of light seeped out from beneath some inner door. Brandon slid in with the stealth of a snake. Standing rigid outside the door of the inner room, he bent his ears to the woodwork. From inside came an irregular tapping noise. The humming note formed a steady, unchanging background to it. Understanding dawned on Brandon.

Holding his spear in one hand, he eased forward and grasped the handle of the door, turning it silently. A crack appeared as he pressed against it. The tapping noise grew more distinct. Opening the door a fraction more, he peered inside. The bearded man sat with his back to Brandon. He wore a pair of headphones over his ears and his rifle was propped against the wall, while one of his hands was constantly moving as he worked a radio key.

Brandon stepped in through the door without fear of being heard. He crept up behind the man's chair and paused, a faintly sardonic smile on his hard mouth.

'That'll be enough!' he said suddenly. At the same time he thrust the spear over the man's shoulder and dug it straight into the intricate bowels of the radio transformer.

The bearded man gave a roar of fury, whirling round to face his visitor. With a lunge, Brandon stepped clear, draggi~ the spear with him. The man ~ sideways for his rifle. Brandon him with an out-thrust boot, then smashed a fist in his face as he sprawled. The radio set went on humming. His effort at putting it out of action had not been successful. But the bearded man was intent on killing him if he could. Brandon kicked his hand away as it almost grasped the rifle. The man gave a dull bellow of rage and pain, then came in, arms flailing. Brandon met the sudden assault with the spear.

The bearded man tried to knock it aside, gripping the shaft just behind the blade. Brandon smashed a fist in his chest. He stumbled forward. The shaft of the spear struck the ground and jammed in the beaten earth of the floor. Red Beard uttered a fearful cry as he ran himself clean through the stomach.

Brandon stood for a moment staring down at him. Then he rolled the body over with his foot. The spear had passed through the man completely, his own weight driving it in as he fell.

'You lost,' said Brandon bleakly.

Glazed eyes stared up at him. Bloodless lips moved, but no sound came. The bearded man died where he lay. Brandon went across to the radio transmitter and examined it. He tried it out, found it to be in working order, and tuned in to the Ruchuru wavelength. Slowly and laboriously he called up the station, using a small microphone attachment he found plugged in. There was no need for key work at this short range.

'Rex Brandon here,' he said quietly. 'I am reporting the closing down of the secret radio in the Congo jungle. Also the death of foreign operator. That is all; we shall be returning to Ruchuru as soon as possible. We will also be bringing Glory Fanshawe with us.'

The operator at Ruchuru gave a gasp, then checked back the message dutifully. When he had finished, he said: 'Oh, by the way, Mr. Brandon, I've a cable for you here. Shall I read it out?'

'Go ahead.'

'To Rex Brandon, Africa. Circus tamer you enquire about missing from England after losing licence for assault and cruelty. Present whereabouts unknown, but marvellous trainer. Thought to be a foreigner, though nationality dubious. Let me know if you find him. Will sign him up for a tour anytime. Martin.'

Brandon grinned sourly. 'Thanks,' he said, 'but Martin won't want to sign up dead meat, I'm afraid.'

'What's that you say?' stammered the operator.

'Nothing, my lad. Thanks a lot. Good-bye.'

He stood up, glanced round, and then left the bungalow, to disappear in the darkness as he made his way to re-join the others at the edge of the swamp.

'All settled,' he said. 'I've even reported to base.'

They started off on the long trek home, meeting a dozen of the U.N. police force on the following day. These men carried on, and later returned to Ruchuru with loads of material discovered in an arms dump near the jungle hut.

*   *   *

Brandon was sipping a long whisky and soda on McNulty's veranda one night a week afterwards. Glory Fanshawe was there, as well as Graham.

'Wasn't bad fun while it lasted, was it?' he murmured. 'We stopped it just in time, from what I gather.'

'Wizard show!' enthused Graham, stroking his moustache.

Glory shuddered violently. 'If it hadn't been for you boys, I'd have died,' she said.

'Glad we came along,' murmured Brandon. He caught McNulty's eye and winked. The two of them sauntered off for an evening stroll, leaving Graham and Glory alone on the cool veranda.

Graham watched them go. 'Bang on!' he drawled. 'Let's you and I have another drink.'

She nodded, smiling in a way which her public never saw on the silver screen.

We do hope that you have enjoyed reading this large print book.

Did you know that all of our titles are available for purchase?

We publish a wide range of high quality large print books including:
Romances, Mysteries, Classics
General Fiction
Non Fiction and Westerns

Special interest titles available in large print are:
The Little Oxford Dictionary
Music Book, Song Book
Hymn Book, Service Book

Also available from us courtesy of Oxford University Press:
Young Readers' Dictionary
(large print edition)
Young Readers' Thesaurus
(large print edition)

For further information or a free brochure, please contact us at:
Ulverscroft Large Print Books Ltd.,
The Green, Bradgate Road, Anstey,
Leicester, LE7 7FU, England.
Tel: (00 44) **0116 236 4325**
Fax: (00 44) **0116 234 0205**

VICTIMS OF EVIL

Victor Rousseau

A gang led by the mysterious Doctor Omega is targeting prominent New York financiers for blackmail. One victim arranges a police trap for the criminals — which fails. Revenge is swift and brutal. The defiant financier is assaulted by an unseen hand in a peculiar and gruesome manner, left unconscious and bleeding from his left eye. When he wakes, the full horror of the attack becomes apparent. For the man is still alive, but left babbling gibberish and unable to communicate . . .

THE TWELVE APOSTLES

Gerald Verner

Under the light of a full moon, amid the sinister ruins of an ancient abbey, a man gasps out his last breath as he lies in a pool of his own blood. Who, amongst the residents of the sleepy little village, has a motive for the murder? And how is it connected to twelve silver statues of the apostles, missing for centuries, and the enigmatic Abbot's Key mentioned in a criminal's dying words? Superintendent Budd is called in to solve one of his most baffling cases.

THE LIBRARY DETECTIVE

James Holding

Hal Johnson is a retired cop who works for his city's public library, tracking down missing and overdue books. But his switch of careers is no sinecure, for his work always seems to lead him into some sort of mystery, such as blackmail, robbery, kidnapping — and even murder. In the course of collecting fines and recovering books, Hal finds himself in plenty of dangerous situations that require him to use all his former police skills . . .

WITNESS TO MURDER

Norman Firth

Through her window, June Merrill idly watches her neighbour in the adjoining flats — only to see her being suddenly, savagely killed. Having watched murder being committed, June knows that she, as the only witness, is now in mortal danger . . . In *Message from a Stranger*, Mike Carr watches a beautiful woman across a restaurant. Just before she leaves with two strange men, she scrawls a cryptic note in lipstick on the table-cloth — which Mike must decipher to save her from danger . . .

THIS IS THE HOUSE

Shelley Smith

On a picturesque West Indies island, the capital is dominated by the house on the mountaintop: the house that Jacques built. Premier Justice Antoine Jacques was divinely happy with his beautiful wife Julia and their son Raoul — until Julia was stricken with total paralysis . . . For years now, La Morte, as she is known, has been confined to her bed. Then, one day, she is found dead. And Quentin Seal, author of detective stories, is begged by Antoine to investigate . . .

THE SNARK WAS A BOOJUM

Gerald Verner and Chris Verner

When William Baker is found dead, his naked and twisted body lying under a bench in the dingy waiting room of a train station, the village police are baffled. Soon afterward another corpse appears, this time posthumously stuffed into full evening dress, with black pigment smeared on his face. A murderer is at large whose M.O. is to use his victims to recreate scenes from Lewis Carroll's nonsense poem, 'The Hunting of the Snark' — and it's up to amateur detective Simon Gale to stop him before he kills again.